COWBOY CLASSIFIEDS

Cowboy Seeking a City Girl

JANICE WHITEAKER

Cowboy Seeking a City Girl, a prequel of the Cowboys of Moss Creek series

www.janicewhiteaker.com

First printing, 2022

CHAPTER ONE

MARYANN STARED ACROSS the dirt-covered space, holding her breath as the wind shifted, whipping the thick scent of animal and manure directly across her face.

Again.

"You look unhappy." Cliff was decked out in a ridiculous ensemble. One that included a pair of over-pressed blue jeans and a starched shirt sporting an indecent amount of fringe. He looked as out of place as she felt.

But at least she didn't come dressed like a rhinestone cowboy.

Maryann glanced away from Cliff's absurd outfit just in time to dodge a burly man on his way to the metal bleachers, an overflowing beer and a plate of dripping nachos gripped tight in his hands. Unfortunately, side-stepping him meant moving closer to the dingy building on the other side of the dusty path they were walking. She quickly caught the skirt of her favorite dress and held it close, keeping the pale blue fabric from brushing against the filthy wood siding. "I'm fine." She plastered on a smile, hoping it looked convincing.

Cliff was, by all accounts, a good catch. The kind of guy she should be happy to be spending her Friday night with.

He was attractive. Well-spoken. Smart. A decent conversationalist. And poised to take a position at his family's firm once he graduated from law school.

But for some reason, she was having to work harder and harder to talk herself into accepting another date with him.

And tonight was probably a good example of why that was happening.

"You sure?" Cliff was already on the move again, not bothering to wait for the reassurance he didn't really want.

Because at the end of the day, Cliff was also kind of an ass.

So far he'd taken her to a concert for one of his favorite musicians—someone she'd never even heard of before—and to his favorite seafood restaurant, even though she'd told him at least ten times about her shellfish allergy.

And now she was here. Standing in the middle of a dirt field, waiting in line to pick out her dinner from a list of items scribbled across poster board in barely legible writing.

It was... disappointing.

"I need to use the bathroom." Maryann stepped out

of the concession line, thinking Cliff would do the same.

Her bladder was actually fine.

She just needed a minute to get her thoughts together.

Wrap her head around how she'd failed to notice that Cliff wasn't really interested in developing a relationship with her.

All he wanted was someone at his side, keeping him from having to do whatever he wanted to do alone. She was nothing more than a captive companion, one lured in by the package he presented.

"Okay." Cliff didn't even glance in her direction. All his focus stayed on the menu.

If you could call it that.

At least nothing on the list held the possibility of sending her to the hospital this time, so she might still rank it higher than the Seafood Palace.

"I guess I'll be back." Maryann took another step away from the line, still hoping Cliff might offer to help her find the location of the facilities.

Maybe ask what she wanted from the concession stand.

Hell, some sort of an acknowledgment that she was there.

But Cliff offered none of it.

He was too excited about this *special evening* he'd planned for them.

Right.

Maryann huffed out an annoyed laugh as she finally turned away, giving up on Cliff in more than one way.

This *special evening* definitely wasn't for *them*. Like every other place he'd taken her to, this one was only for Cliff.

It was a disappointing realization to make, especially in the middle of what was turning out to be one hell of a crowded rodeo.

The crowd seemed to be getting thicker by the second, and everyone appeared just as excited about the evening as Cliff was, making it next to impossible to move. She couldn't even blame the pumps on her feet for her inability to navigate her way out of the situation.

So maybe she was the problem. That was always how it seemed to go.

She was the one always finding fault with every man who took her out. Every man who expressed any sort of interest.

And now here she was again.

Struggling to find the good in an evening she should probably be enjoying.

But this evening wasn't for her. Not even a little bit.

And maybe that was too much to ask. Maybe hoping for a man who might think of her every once in a while was more than she should expect.

Maryann passed a group of women about her age, watching as the trio giggled and pointed, leaning to whisper into each other's ears as they made their way toward the grandstand. She turned as they passed, wondering what in the hell she was missing.

They looked thrilled to be here. Excited about an

evening she was heavily considering abandoning.

Except she wasn't the one who drove, and Cliff certainly wasn't going to be interested in leaving, so she'd have to find another way home.

Amanda would probably be happy to come pick her up. Her roommate wasn't the biggest fan of Cliff's anyway. She would probably love the opportunity to whisk Maryann away from yet another self-serving evening.

Then they could go back to their apartment, she could put on her pajamas, and sit on the couch to sulk over another man biting the dating dust.

All she had to do was find a payphone.

Maryann pushed up onto her toes, trying to see through the clog of bodies cutting any sort of visibility down to nothing.

"You look lost."

It took her a second to realize the slow drawl and deep voice were directed at her.

Maryann turned toward what she hoped might be an offer of help. "I'm just looking for the—" Her words died in her throat, strangled off at the sight of the first man to show any concern about her welfare tonight.

She might be starting to have an idea about what had those women so excited to be at the rodeo.

It wasn't the horses.

It wasn't the bulls.

And it definitely wasn't the food.

It was the cowboys.

Cowboys like the one watching her with cool, blue

eyes.

He was tall with broad shoulders that filled out the blue button-down shirt stretched across his chest in ways she didn't realize were possible. His well-worn jeans fit his lower half so well it was practically indecent.

Add in the boots and the hat, and the man was more than worthy of the giggling, pointing, and whispering she saw earlier.

"You're looking for the *what*? I couldn't really hear you over all the noise." He stepped closer, bringing along the scent of leather and spice. "But I'll be happy to help you find whatever it is you're looking for."

"Um." Maryann cleared her throat, trying to find her train of thought.

But all she seemed to be finding was more new places to stare at on the cowboy in front of her.

The square cut of his jaw.

The line of a dimple that probably peeked out when he smiled.

The fullness of his lips as they quirked into what might be considered a smirk.

Everything about him was shockingly fascinating.

It was probably just because he was a novelty. So different from the men she'd been weeding through for the past year, thinking she might manage to find Mr. Right before graduating from college.

As graduation was done and over with, she'd clearly missed that chance.

But she was having a hard time being too upset about it right now, because the smirk she was anticipating bloomed into a full-fledged smile that revealed that damn dimple she knew was there. And it sent Maryann's stomach flipping to her toes.

"I'm not so sure where the *um* is, but I'd be happy to escort you around the property while we look for it." He crooked his arm in her direction, an offer Maryann should absolutely reject.

She came here with Cliff. On a date.

An admittedly self-centered one he clearly planned only for himself.

Just like all the ones that came before it.

But still.

She should go find him, and at least be polite enough to let him know she was planning to leave.

Except finding Cliff on her own would be tricky. She could easily spend an hour hiking from one end of the arena to the other without crossing his path.

And this cowboy seemed to be familiar with the area, so it only made sense to accept his help.

Maryann smiled. Not that it was difficult to do considering who was smiling back at her. "Thank you. I got a little turned around." She slid her hand into his offered arm, curving it around the thick swell of his bicep.

The man had an actual bicep. One her fingers itched to squeeze, just a little, to see if it was as solid as it seemed.

But she wouldn't do that.

That's not what this was about. He was simply going to help her find...

Cliff. He was going to help her find Cliff.

"It can be easy to get turned around in these places." The cowboy pointed to an area just along the aging wood fence surrounding the entirety of the property, leaning close so she could hear him over the drone of everything around them. "Let's get out of the middle of this crowd so you can tell me where it is you want to go."

Maryann nodded. "Okay."

It was the smart thing to do. Out here in the middle of everything was chaotic and noisy and congested. It only made sense to go someplace a little quieter.

So it would be easier to hear the slow way words seemed to roll off his tongue.

The cowboy kept her tucked in close at his side as he expertly navigated the crowd. It was impressive to watch, the way he used his broad shoulders and tall frame to part the never-ending stream of bodies coming their way.

Unfortunately, since her eyes accidentally stayed on the cowboy, they weren't watching the uneven ground.

Which meant Maryann didn't see the dip in the dirt until it was too late.

"Oop." The heel of her shoe went one way as her foot tried to go another, threatening to send Maryann stumbling into the mass of people herding toward the stands.

"I've got you." The cowboy wrapped one arm around her waist, catching her before she could even fully lose her footing. He gave her a wink and an easy smile. "The terrain here can be a little tricky to negotiate."

Maryann huffed out a breath, embarrassment over

her obviously incorrect wardrobe choices making her feel the need to explain. "I didn't realize this was where I was going to be when I got dressed."

"I could have guessed that." The cowboy cleared the last of the crowd, using his arm around her waist to direct her to the most level spot along the fence. The second she was steady on her feet his hands left her body.

Which was surprisingly disappointing considering how disappointing the night was in general.

The cowboy leaned one shoulder against the fence, looking completely relaxed and at home in a place she would never have set foot in on her own volition.

Maryanne glanced toward the grandstand before turning back his way. "Are you one of the cowboys from the rodeo?"

He tipped his head in a small nod. "I am." He held one hand out between them. "Billy Pace."

Maryann glanced down at his hand. It was as big and solid as the rest of him. She swallowed hard as she reached out to take it, knowing there was a good chance she might spend the rest of her life comparing every man's hand to this specific man's hand.

It was wide and warm and rough in a way that almost made her shiver.

Unfortunately, it was attached to the kind of man she had zero experience with.

She'd spent her college years dating pale men with smooth hands and fat wallets, wondering why none of them did much of anything for her.

Now she knew.

"Maryann Morgan." It took everything she had to pull her hand from his, but it was the decent thing to do.

Not that she'd been acting particularly decent up until now.

Which was silly. This man was with the rodeo. That meant he wasn't from here.

He'd be gone in the blink of an eye, never to be seen or heard from again.

Definitely not the long-term situation she was seeking.

Billy edged in a little closer. "What brings you to the rodeo on a Friday night, Miss Maryann?"

It wasn't easy to immediately admit the truth, which was one more bit of silliness.

"I came here on a date." She forced it out.

There was no reason to try to hide Cliff or the fact that their final date together was what brought her to the Stars and Stripes Rodeo.

And this would definitely be their final date.

Billy's brows lifted. "Interesting." His eyes skimmed down her knee-length, belted dress. "And he didn't have the decency to let you know you were coming to the rodeo?"

Maryann shook her head. "I thought we were going out to dinner."

Billy clicked his tongue, eyes holding hers. "Seems a shame for you to put all that work into gettin' dressed up and then no one takes you to dinner."

CHAPTER TWO

HE DIDN'T HAVE time to take this woman wherever it was she needed to be on the property, let alone out to dinner.

But that was just a small technicality.

One he was happy to overlook.

Maryann's brows lifted, creeping up toward the dork blonde line of her bangs. "Are you offering to take me out to dinner?"

"I am." He shouldn't be.

But he'd been traveling for almost six months and the idea of spending just one meal across from Maryann Morgan was getting more appealing by the second.

She looked down his front, her eyes moving a little faster than the last few times she'd done it. "What about the rodeo? Don't you have to ride a horse or something?"

She was clearly out of her element here. Maybe that was what made her so appealing to him.

He was used to women chasing him around, hoping for a night with a cowboy.

His friends loved the attention being in the rodeo earned them. Took full advantage of the opportunities it presented.

But that wasn't really what he was looking for.

Not that he really knew what he was looking for.

"I do have to go ride a horse or something." Billy checked his watch. "But I can be done in a half an hour." He was early in the lineup. A few seconds on the back of a bronco and they could be on their way.

As long as he didn't take a hoof to the face.

Maryann glanced toward the grandstand again, looking cautious.

It made sense. She didn't know him from Adam.

"How about this," he tipped his head toward the door leading to the private area at the back of the outdoor arena, "you can think about it while you wait for me to do my thing." Billy crossed both arms over his chest, trying to look relaxed. "Once I'm done you can decide if we go out to dinner," he shot her a wink, "or if we eat from the concession stand."

The options didn't seem to put Maryann any more at ease.

He wanted her to be comfortable with him, but his resources for making that happen were limited.

Almost as limited as his time.

"I'll introduce you to my friends. They can tell you the worst thing I'll do is steal food off your plate."

"It's not that." Maryann shifted on her feet. "I just feel bad because I came here with someone else."

The admission shouldn't make him as happy as it did, but it was nice to know her problem wasn't with him. "Doesn't seem like he's too worried about you." Billy glanced around, looking for any sign of the man who should have stayed right by Maryann's side.

He brought her to a crowded arena filled with half-drunk spectators who were already wound tight and ready for excitement. And then he either left her to do his own thing or didn't even bother to notice she'd walked away from him.

Maryann stuck out like a sore thumb here and from the sound of it, this was the last place she expected to be tonight. She looked uncomfortable as hell when he came across her, and her date should have noticed that and done whatever it took to take care of her.

But he didn't.

So that left room for someone else to do it.

Maryann huffed out a little breath as her eyes searched the crowd. "I'm pretty sure that's not something he's capable of."

"If he's not worried about you then I think that means you don't have to worry about him." Billy smiled, trying to look less invested in her answer than he was. "Those are the rules."

Maryann gave him a small smile back. "I think I might need you to get me a copy of those rules." Her eyes dropped between them. "I'm not so good at following them."

The announcer's voice cut through the static on the speakers, encouraging everyone to find their seat, which meant his time was running out.

Normally he couldn't wait for the evening to start. To get out in front of the crowd and show them what he was capable of.

But right now all he cared about was showing this woman. There was something about her. The way she still stood tall even when the night wasn't going the way she hoped.

He'd lied when he first spoke to her. She didn't look lost. She might have been searching for something, but nothing about the lift of her chin or the straightness of her spine looked lost.

Which made him wonder how in the hell the man she came with didn't realize what he had and do everything in his power to make sure she stayed his. "You been dating this guy long?"

Maryann shook her head, sending the soft curls around her head swinging. "Maybe a month." She lifted one shoulder. "We've gone out five or six times." She let out a sigh. "He's not a bad person, just..." Her eyes drifted away again.

Billy resisted the urge to move closer to her. "Just?"

She sighed again as she readjusted the purse over one shoulder. "Just really focused on what interests him."

That explained how she ended up here. Made him wonder where she'd ended up on the other five dates. "What interests you?"

Maryann's eyes jumped to his. "What?"

"I asked what interests you." From the way it sounded Maryann Morgan wasn't looking to be wined and dined.

She just wanted someone to think about her once in a while.

"Well..." She reached up to slide her hair behind one ear. "I just got a degree in business management."

"And that's what interests you? Business management?"

"I mean, it's a useful degree. I'll be able to find all kinds of jobs with it." She was immediately defensive, making him wonder who'd given her a hard time about her career choice.

Probably the same guy who abandoned her at the rodeo.

"Makes sense to me." Billy frowned the announcer came back across the speakers, offering up the countdown that used to get his blood pumping with anticipation.

But right now it was really fucking up his plans.

Maryann's gaze lifted to the speaker above their head. "Are you going to be late?"

"Probably." He offered up the truth.

Maryann fiddled with the strap of her purse. "Well," she glanced from him to the gate marked with a fading PRIVATE sign, "where do you have to go?"

Billy tipped his head toward the very gate she was looking at. "Right through there." He let himself move in a little closer even though most of the crowd was long gone. "You're more than welcome to come with me."

Maryann chewed her lower lip. “Are you sure I’m allowed?”

He managed to hold back a smile. “Positive.”

He wasn’t positive, but what in the hell would they do? Kick her out?

Wouldn’t happen. Not unless they wanted to kick him out too.

And he brought in way too many people for them to kick him out.

Maryann was quiet for a few long seconds, each one dragging out for what felt like an eternity.

Finally her eyes came to his. “Okay.”

He let out a breath he didn’t realize he’d been holding. “Okay then.” Billy straightened away from the fence, offering his arm again. “Let’s get this show on the road.”

She let out a breathy laugh, but slid her hand into place, fingers squeezing tight as they walked over the patchy grass. “And what all does this show involve?”

“Tonight?” Billy took his time leading her to the fence, knowing the second she crossed into his world he would have to fight for every bit of her attention. “Tonight’s the riding night.”

“Riding night?” Maryann seemed genuinely interested, which probably explained how she ended up with a man who didn’t seem all that interested in her.

“Riding night.” Billy scanned the space one final time, looking for any sign that Maryann’s date came to his senses and realized she wasn’t coming back.

But there was no one rushing their direction.

And Maryann didn’t seem concerned about it at all.

Every bit of her attention was focused on him. "So that's what you do? Ride?"

"That's what I do." And for the first time in his life he wanted to get it the hell over with so he could spend the rest of the night finding out what actually interested Maryann Morgan.

Because he was willing to bet all his winnings that it wasn't business management.

Billy opened the gate, letting Maryann pass through first before following her in and closing it behind them.

This particular rodeo was the biggest one in the state of California, and the three-day affair pulled in spectators from all over the state to come watch men and women from across the country compete for high-dollar prizes.

It's what brought him here. The high he'd been chasing for almost five years while he put off the life waiting for him.

"Oh, wow." Maryann scooted in closer at his side as she stared at the scene around them with wide eyes.

The space behind the fence was just as crowded as the other side, only this side wasn't just full of people. Horses and bulls were organized into stalls and corrals, marked and waiting for their own turn in the arena.

"This way." Billy kept her close as they wove their way through a crowd for the second time.

He almost made it to the line of bleachers reserved for the folks behind the scenes before one of his friends came out of nowhere.

"Where in the hell have you been?" Dale's eyes found

their way to Maryann. His face worked into a slow smile. "Well, well, well."

"Shut it." Billy shot him a glare. "Where's everybody else?"

"Where you're supposed to be." Dale's smile was still out and his eyes stayed on Maryann. "Gettin' ready." His attention finally came Billy's way. "Aren't you gonna introduce me to your new friend?"

Billy shouldered past his traveling buddy. "No."

He pulled Maryann along with him as he made his way toward the space reserved for riders and their gear. He led her into the booth where the rest of his friends were strapping into their chaps and vests. Almost in unison the group looked up, all their attention immediately going to the woman at his side.

He couldn't blame them. Maryann was easy on the eyes.

But that wasn't why they all looked as shocked as they did.

"Holy shit." Justin's jaw dropped open. "It's about fucking time."

"Shut it." Billy cut Justin off with the same words he used on Dale. He was probably going to have to repeat them five hundred more times before the night was over. "Where's everyone sitting?"

"We've got a section in the stands." Justin finished buttoning his vest. "I'd be happy to escort your lady friend there."

"Not happening." Billy grabbed his chaps and vest.

"You're gonna fuck around and miss your call." Jerry,

one of the older members of their crew tipped his head toward the arena. "Go. I'll make sure she gets where she needs to go."

The announcer's voice backed up Jerry's words, sending Billy's eyes to the gates.

For the first time in his life it was the last place he wanted to be.

"I'll be fine." Maryann's smile was strong and sincere. "You go."

Billy glanced at Jerry before pulling Maryann closer, lowering his voice as he held her gaze. "I don't want to go."

Her eyes barely widened. "But this is what you came here for."

Technically she was right.

He'd worked hard to get here, fighting his way to the top to secure his spot at one of the most elite rodeos in the west.

But it seemed less important than it did when he woke up this morning.

Maryann smiled. "You only have to stay on a few seconds, right?"

"Right." He pulled in a long breath. "I won't be gone long."

Maryann glanced at where a group of cowboys were looking their way. "I'm not worried." Her lips twisted into a little smirk. "It seems like I might have plenty of entertainment while you're gone."

Billy shot the group of men a warning glare. "That's what I'm worried about."

CHAPTER THREE

"YOU EVER BEEN to something like this before?" The older man sitting right beside her kept his eyes on the arena.

Maryann shook her head. "No."

And honestly, up until the last few minutes, she'd been regretting being here tonight.

But maybe her initial assessment of the event was premature.

Or possibly tainted by the initial companion that led her here.

"You know what he's about to do?" Jerry was probably just a little younger than her father. He had a slow drawl, just like Billy's, and the same easy smile.

Not that she was seeing it right now.

"He's about to ride a horse, right?" Her knowledge of the way this event worked was limited at best.

She knew cowboys rode horses. Sometimes bulls. They used lassos, and spurs, and—

"He's about to get on a horse that wants nothing more than to kick his ass right back off it." Jerry's eyes finally came her direction. "And he's gonna do it without a saddle."

"Bareback?"

Jerry's greying brows lifted in surprise, like he couldn't believe she knew that word. "Yup. Bareback."

The way he said it almost seemed ominous and it made her stomach clench. "Is that good, or bad?"

"Depends on how many brain cells you like in a man." Jerry's crinkled eyes went back to the dirt floor at the center of the arena. "Because he's about to lose a few of them." His head tipped to one side. "And maybe a couple of teeth."

"So what he's about to do is dangerous?" Shock and concern made her question the obvious.

Of course it was dangerous. Billy was about to get on a bucking horse with no saddle to hang onto.

That wasn't a safe way to pass time.

She just didn't realize it was *lose brain cells and teeth* dangerous.

Luckily Jerry didn't seem interested in pointing out the idiocy of her question. His gaze was firmly fixed on the gates in front of them.

A second later a loud clang sent Maryann jumping in her seat, pulling her purse closer to her chest as the announcer's voice started to wail out through the speakers. A beautiful horse came bounding out into the open space of the arena. The man on his back almost looked like he was lying flat, the whole front of his body facing up at the sky. Maryann held her breath, fingers gripping the leather of her purse.

It felt like forever as she watched, seconds ticking past like hours, unable to blink as her gut twisted tighter and tighter.

Then it was done, leaving her staring open mouthed as everyone around her cheered.

And that probably included Cliff, wherever he was.

The cowboy gimped his way across the dirt, looking like he'd just had the literal shit beat out of him.

"Why do they do that?" She struggled to wrap her brain around the appeal.

She liked her brain cells just as much as she liked her teeth. Neither was worth risking on the back of an angry horse.

"They do it for all kinds of reasons." Jerry shrugged. "Some of them good, some of them bad."

Maryann studied the man at her side. "Why does Billy do it?"

"The second part." He leaned back in his seat, crossing his arms. "But you didn't hear that from me."

Interesting.

Which was exactly what this night was turning out to be.

Certainly the most interesting thing Cliff had ever invited her to.

And that had nothing to do with Cliff and everything to do with the cowboy that was about to have his prefrontal cortex banged against his skull.

Maryann scooted closer to the edge of her seat with

each horse that broke free of the gate. By the time the fifth cowboy was up she was grateful as heck that she hadn't managed to make it through the concession stand line, because anything that might still be in her stomach was churning around, stirred by a nervous energy she couldn't contain.

There was no reason to be nervous. She didn't know Billy. Didn't have any clue how many brain cells he may or may not be able to spare.

But the thought of him getting hurt made it hard to take a deep breath.

"Billy's a good man." Jerry didn't look at her when he said it. "I just thought you should know."

"Oh." Maryann gave him a little smile even though his gaze was firmly planted at the center of the arena. "Okay."

She wasn't really sure what else to say.

Billy might be a good man, but she was beginning to question whether or not he was a smart man.

Because what smart man would willingly get on the back of a horse, risking life, limb, and molars, all for a little bit of what?

Notoriety? Fame? Adoration?

The last one made the most sense, because there was no shortage of admiration around here.

Women were lined up everywhere, all batting their eyes and pursing their lips at every cowboy that walked past.

Not that she could really blame them. There was

definitely something about the right man in boots and jeans that did strange things to a woman.

The worry currently turning her inside out was evidence of that.

Maryann's heart jumped to her throat as a familiar name was announced across the speakers.

"Up next is the evening's favorite, Billy Pace."

Her head snapped to the man still at her side. "The evening's favorite?"

Jerry didn't acknowledge her question. He probably didn't hear it since all his attention was focused on the gates.

Which sent Maryann's attention racing there as well. Her eyes found Billy's easily. He sat taller than everyone around him, watching her from the back of a beautiful black horse.

A horse that was about to do its best to slam the sense out of him.

And, based on that fact alone, the amount of sense he had to spare might be slim to none.

She sat up straighter in her seat, air freezing in her lungs as the countdown started. By the time the gate opened, both hands were over her mouth, fingers pressing into her skin as she watched Billy's long, strong body bounce around.

It was horrifying.

Every muscle in her body started to clench, like she could help hold him on the back of the horse.

Not that she was sure that was the better option,

because being on the back of the horse looked just as painful as hitting the ground would be.

The second time was called all the air rushed from her body, racing faster as Jerry jumped to his feet beside her, clapping and hollering with a level of excitement that was shocking.

So Billy must have done a good job, whatever that meant.

He'd stayed on the back of the horse the whole time, but so far everyone had. The rules of this thing must be based on more than just the ability to not fall on your ass, because a set of judges across the way had been dishing out scores that seemed random and arbitrary at best.

Maryann went to her feet since that's what pretty much everyone around her was doing. She grabbed hold of Jerry's shirt, yanking him close so he could hear her over the roar of the crowd. "Did he do well?"

Jerry was still clapping and cheering. "*That is how you do it.*" He wasn't talking to her, but still effectively answered her question.

Apparently, Billy had obviously done the horse-riding thing much better than the man before him. What made his ride better was completely lost on her, but she still felt a strange sense of pride.

So for the first time in a long time, she just went with it.

Maryann braced her hands on each side of her mouth and hooted along with Jerry. Then she hooked two fingers between her lips and let out a loud whistle.

Jerry turned her way, giving her a slow nod of approval as he continued to clap.

She grinned back at him, feeling a little more comfortable in this foreign world.

After a few minutes, the cheering died down and everyone dropped back to their seats. Maryann let out a long breath, feeling like she had way more invested in those few seconds then she actually did. “So now he’s done? That was it?”

“Now he waits to see how everyone else does.” Jerry was back to his serious self. “Then they tally up all the scores and announce the winners.”

“When does that happen?” Billy told her he would be done soon and then they could go.

“Not for a few hours.”

“Hours?” She glanced at her watch. It was already seven. In a few more hours it would be well past dinner, and no place would be open.

“I’m going to get something to drink.” Jerry leaned her way. “You want anything?”

“No, thank you.” Maryann offered as much of a smile as she could manage. “I’m fine.”

Maybe she misunderstood Billy’s plan. Or maybe he just had a terrible sense of time.

Or maybe he was just like Cliff, good at making things sound like they might be fun for her, when in reality her enjoyment didn’t matter at all.

Maryann slumped down in her seat, a little more disappointed than she should be over the possibility.

"You ready to go, darlin'?" Billy's voice sent her spinning toward the seat Jerry vacated.

He was stretched out in the small space, legs taking up every inch of available property as he watched her with an easy smile.

"We can't go. You don't know if you won yet." She wasn't pouting about it, really she wasn't.

Billy's easy smile widened. "You sure about that?" He held one hand in her direction. "Let's go get you that dinner you deserve."

Maryann glanced back toward the arena. "But what happens if you win and you're not here?"

Billy shrugged. "Don't know."

"I think that's something you should probably find out before we just leave." A minute ago she was almost upset that maybe Billy wasn't all she was starting to hope he was.

But now she realized this man was willing to walk away from a possible win, and whatever that entailed, to take her out to dinner.

And honestly, she wasn't sure which possibility bothered her more.

Billy leaned closer, his big body crowding her space in the most appealing way. "I have won plenty of these, Miss Maryann." He reached out to run the tip of one finger along the line of her jaw. "But I've never taken you out to dinner." He was so close that his face was all she could see. "And I believe that will make for a much more rewarding evening than this place ever could."

"I think you did do some brain cells in." Maryann glanced around, catching more than a few adoring eyes directed at the man beside her. "What do you win?"

Billy shrugged. "Nothing I haven't won before."

It was strange to actually be arguing to stay at the rodeo she didn't want to be at not so long ago. "Which is?"

Billy tipped his head to one side. "Just a little money."

He was acting way too nonchalant about this, and it was making her suspicious. "How much money is a little money?"

Billy hesitated. "I think it's ten thousand."

Her jaw dropped open. Literally. "If you win then you get ten thousand dollars?"

She was expecting maybe a few hundred. Possibly a trophy.

But ten thousand dollars?

"That's first place. Second place is only five."

Maryann pressed one hand to her head. "Did you just say only five, as in only five thousand dollars?" It was money he had a strong possibility of winning. Money that might not be his if he wasn't here to claim it. "We have to stay."

"I don't think we do." Billy was shockingly relaxed about the possibility of walking away from thousands of dollars.

"Absolutely, we do. You might not get your money if we leave." Dinner was great and all, but ten thousand dollars was ten thousand dollars. Billy could buy himself a lot of dinners with that.

Not that he seemed to care.

He leaned in even closer, one arm resting against the back of her seat. “But I might not get you if we stay.”

CHAPTER FOUR

HE THOUGHT MARYANN would be flattered by the fact that he was willing to give up whatever proceeds of this event might find their way into his pocket in favor of spending time with her.

Instead, she was looking at him like he had three heads.

Finally, she shook her head. "Nope. Absolutely not." She scooted back in her seat, like she was settling in. "We're staying here."

"I thought you wanted to go out to dinner?" He was more than a little confused. "That's what you got all dressed up for."

"Well now I've changed my mind." Maryann faced the arena, watching the next rider like she was invested in his performance. "Now I want to stay here."

"Maybe I don't." He wanted to go someplace quiet. Someplace where Maryann's attention would belong only to him.

But more than that, he wanted to give her the night she thought she was getting in the first place.

And sitting in a hard seat surrounded by dusty cowboys was definitely not it.

Maryann slowly turned his way. “So you’re suggesting we should do what you want?”

Billy opened his mouth to argue, but immediately clamped it shut again.

Somehow, she’d managed to turn this whole thing around on him. “I’m not the only one who wanted to go to dinner.” He motioned to her dress and shoes. “You picked your whole outfit because that’s where you thought you were going.”

“Well now I changed my mind.” Maryann gave him a sweet smile that looked much more innocent than he suspected she was. “And isn’t it a woman’s prerogative to change her mind?” Her head tipped to one side as she continued to smile his way.

She had him and she knew it.

There was no arguing her logic. Not in any way that would end well for him.

And maybe that wasn’t a bad thing.

“Fine.” Billy leaned back in his seat. “That gives me plenty of time to talk you into letting me take you out for dinner tomorrow night instead.”

He wasn’t giving up on the fancy dinner he promised. It was how he could show her that while he might be a little rough around the edges, he had just as much to offer as whatever city boy brought her here.

Possibly more.

Maryann's smile widened, lighting her whole face up along with it. "I don't think you'll need much time at all to talk me into that."

They were barely an hour into knowing each other and this woman was already surprising him.

"The only problem with that plan is that you still haven't had dinner tonight." Billy couldn't make himself look away from her, even as the crowd around them made it clear he was facing some stiff competition. "And I don't like the idea of you going hungry."

"I doubt I'll starve to death over one skipped meal." Maryann was less successful at ignoring what was happening in the arena and her wide eyes slowly rolled toward the judge's table.

"I'm not worried about you starving." Billy stayed close, making sure all the eyes around them knew Maryann was not available in any way that would be useful to them. "I'm worried about you sitting here suffering over some silly prize."

Her focus came back his way, eyes filled with disbelief. "Some silly prize?" She shook her head. "I would hardly call ten thousand dollars silly."

"Money isn't everything." It sure as hell couldn't buy you happiness. He knew that firsthand because he'd given it one hell of a shot.

"It's not everything, but it is something." Maryann's tone was serious. "Try living without it for a while and let me know if that changes your opinion."

And once again she surprised him. Proving to be more than just the pretty face that reeled him in initially.

There was no doubt in his mind that Maryann was speaking from experience.

And he wanted to know all about it.

But this wasn't the time, or the place.

So he would just have to wait until tomorrow.

"Let's make a deal." Billy checked to see who was next in the lineup. "We've got about twenty minutes to get to the concession stand before it's intermission and everybody and their brother rushes out for another beer and a hot dog." He held her eyes as they met his. "So let's get a move on and go get you something to eat."

It wasn't perfect, and didn't make him happy, but based on the set of her jaw, this was the best he was going to get.

Maryann looked from side to side before finally tipping her head in a little nod. "Deal."

He was going to count that as a win.

Billy stood up, but this time instead of offering his arm he took her hand in his, holding tight as they made their way back out into the public area.

Fifteen minutes later he was loaded down with nachos, hotdogs, popcorn, and anything else they sold. He bought it all, just to be sure Maryann would have whatever she wanted.

She balanced their beers, sticking close at his side as they made their way back to their seats, settling in just as the announcer let everyone know it was intermission.

"That was perfect timing." Maryann reached out to snag a corn chip covered in melted cheese and minced jalapenos. "It's like you've done this before or something."

"Once or twice." Billy grinned as she shoved the cheesy chip into her mouth, managing to get the whole thing in at once.

Maryann wiped at the corner of her mouth before taking a sip of beer. "Have you been doing this a long time?"

Normally he loved talking about the rodeo. Could speak on the subject for hours. It was what interested him most. What his life revolved around.

But he didn't want to admit that to her. Not because she clearly wasn't interested in rodeos in general. He just didn't want to admit the high point of his life was moving from hotel to hotel, chasing prize money and adrenaline.

"Probably a little too long." It was the first time he'd been able to admit it, even though he knew it was true.

Maryann gave him a little smile, wiggling one finger in the direction of his mouth. "Is that because you're worried about all your teeth getting knocked out?"

Billy chuckled. "That should probably be one of the reasons, I suppose."

Maryann leaned in to scan the contents of the large cardboard tray perched across his lap. "But it's not?" She settled on one of the shredded barbecue chicken sandwiches, picking it up and unwrapping the paper around it.

"It is now that I'm thinking about it." Billy snagged

one of the chips, chewing through it as he tried to figure out how to explain the position he was currently in.

Without casting himself in a bad light.

Maryann took a bite of her sandwich, her brows lifting as she started to chew. "This is really good." She chewed a couple more seconds before circling back to the conversation. "So what's the reason that you think you've been doing this a little too long?"

He wasn't surprised that she was willing to cut straight to the chase. He'd only known her a couple of hours, but it was already clear that Maryann was a different kind of person.

One that would keep him on his toes.

"Well," Billy sipped a little of his beer, mulling over how to explain the decisions he'd made.

But there really wasn't a good way to explain it, so he decided to settle on the facts. "My family owns a ranch in Montana, and I'm supposed to take it over when I'm done with the rodeo circuit."

"So you've been dragging your feet." Maryann's lips pressed into a considering line. "Makes sense."

"Does it?" Because, according to his parents, Billy's desire not to immediately jump into running a whole ass ranch didn't make a lick of sense.

"Of course it does." Maryann took another bite of her sandwich. "You wanted to get out and live your life the way you wanted to live it before you go back to live it the way you have to live it." She snagged another nacho. "It's a pretty common thing."

"Is it?" Billy settled on one of the hot dogs, just in

case Maryann could put away her sandwich and still want another one.

"For sure." She huffed out a little laugh. "Pretty much every person I went to college with was doing exactly that."

"Is that what you did?"

Her demeanor changed almost instantly, the lightness she carried settling into a weight he could see.

"I didn't mean to—"

"It's okay." Maryann smiled, but this time it wasn't as bright as before. "I didn't really have the luxury of doing that."

"That's unfortunate." He didn't like the idea of this woman not being able to live the life she dreamt about. Especially when it was clear she would take it by storm.

Maryann shrugged. "I guess that depends on how you look at things."

"How do you look at things?"

Maryann's eyes went across the arena, lingering over the partially empty seats in the grandstand. "I just don't want to worry about the same things my parents have to worry about."

"What is it that your parents have to worry about?"

"Money." Her answer was simple and expected. "My dad isn't very good with it and always manages to burn through everything that finds its way into his pocket." Her eyes jumped to Billy's. "He's not a bad person. Please don't think that's what I'm saying."

"I would never think that." Even in such a short period of time it was obvious that Maryann's father managed to help raise an articulate, kind, confident woman. Any man who could accomplish that couldn't be too bad. "Life is hard. Sometimes you end up chasing whatever makes you happy. Maybe for him that's spending money."

"Is that what you're doing?" Maryann's question was soft. "Chasing what makes you happy?"

He was ashamed to say it was. "Yes."

Her brows came together. "Then why would you want to leave tonight?"

It was a good question. One he didn't have to struggle to answer. "Because I'm thinking there might be other things that will make me even happier."

Maryann's eyes slowly came to his, lifting from where they'd been focused on the tray of nachos.

His answer didn't hide much. And it wasn't that he thought this specific woman could be the key to that kind of happiness, but she was definitely making him realize his days in the rodeo might be numbered.

"Well isn't that the point of life?" Maryann's attention went back to the nachos. "Figuring out how to be happy?"

"Maybe. But I thought I did figure out what made me happy." For years he thought he knew exactly what was important to him.

And most of that time, he'd been right.

But a few months ago things started to change. Every trip seemed longer.

Every rodeo seemed dirtier.

"I'm sure it changes. What made you happy when

you were eighteen isn't the same thing that will make you happy when you're fifty."

Billy laughed a little at that one. "I can't even imagine what will make me happy when I'm fifty."

Maryann's easy smile was back. "I'm willing to bet it's not going to be whatever it was you just did out there today."

"I'm willing to bet my body couldn't handle it even if it was." Billy relaxed a little at the easy way the conversation flowed between them.

In spite of the surprisingly serious nature of it.

Maryann shook her head. "I am one-hundred-percent confident my body couldn't handle it now."

"Not all horseback rides look like the ones you're seeing today." He didn't like that she was getting such a one-sided view of the world he'd grown up in. "There's plenty of horses out there that walk so smooth they'll put you to sleep."

He could imagine Maryann on the back of a horse, her dark blonde hair blowing in the breeze.

Or maybe that was just wishful thinking.

Because somehow, in the course of a couple hours, he managed to go from wanting to take her to dinner, to wanting to take her home.

To Montana.

To show her who he really was.

Because he was starting to think it wasn't really the dumbass kid traveling the country to avoid responsibility.

"I've never ridden a horse." Maryann's cheeks pinked

up just a little. “I’m sure that doesn’t surprise you since I wasn’t originally thrilled to be here tonight.”

It was something he didn’t intend to forget. Especially since she was still sitting at his side, eating concession stand crap instead of the fancy meal he’d hoped to give her. “I won’t take it personally.”

CHAPTER FIVE

"ARE YOU DOING okay?"

Maryann nodded, doing her best to stifle a yawn.

She was exhausted. Between the adrenaline rush of watching Billy bounce around on the back of a horse and the pile of junk food she'd consumed, she was starting to drag.

And it was still the best evening she'd had in a long time.

Billy hadn't left her side all night. He'd stuck right with her, explaining every bit of the events as they watched them unfold, making sure she was never lost or confused about what was happening.

But he didn't just talk about the rodeo.

He told her about Montana. About the ranch his family owned. About the little town of Moss Creek where he grew up.

About the life he had waiting for him.

A life that was very different from the one she envisioned for herself.

She'd expected to find her future husband at college. Assumed they would settle down in the city. Buy a home. Have kids.

The all-American dream.

But was it really?

"They should announce the winners any minute." Billy checked the giant digital clock blinking across the billboard. "Are you sure you don't want to go?"

He'd offered to leave no less than twenty times. Enough that she almost thought he *wanted* to walk out of here.

But she was not going to let that happen, especially since, based on all the chatter around them, it appeared Billy was going to be taking home a first-place win.

Not that he seemed too interested in it.

He'd spent most of the evening completely oblivious to what was going on in the arena. Instead of watching the men he was competing against, he passed the time asking her questions, listening to her answers, and then following up by sharing a little of his own life.

Billy had said more, and certainly listened more, in a few hours than Cliff had in five whole dates.

"Yes, I'm sure I don't want to go." Unfortunately, as soon as the words cleared her lips, the yawn she'd been fighting broke free, making her look like a liar.

She'd been up extra early this morning, trying to get everything ready for the new job she was starting on

Monday, since she was expecting to spend most of her weekend with Cliff.

Which now seemed silly.

She wasn't really that interested in him, and he clearly wasn't that interested in her.

He wasn't a bad guy. Just wrapped up in himself.

"We should go." Billy acted like he was ready to get up. As if he fully intended to whisk her away from this place because of a single yawn.

It was one of the many endearing qualities making Maryann glad she didn't follow through with calling Amanda so her roommate could come to the rescue. "Absolutely not. We are not going until the awards ceremony is over."

Billy was clearly the man of the evening.

She'd gotten more than a few looks from any number of beautiful women. None of them were mean, but they definitely held a decent amount of envy.

Which she didn't blame them for. If the night had shaken out differently, she would have been the one watching some other woman be doted on by a handsome cowboy.

While Cliff ignored her completely.

Billy frowned at her. "You're tired."

"I'm not the one who had their brains scrambled on the back of the horse." Maryann smiled when he scoffed, adding on more reassurance. "I'm fine."

It wasn't a lie. She was fine.

More than fine.

So apparently you could be both tired and more than fine at the same time.

"You better find the nicest restaurant around here, because that's where I'm taking you tomorrow." Billy's expression was comically serious.

Like he thought he owed her for sitting here beside him.

Which couldn't be farther from the truth.

For the first time in forever she'd had a real conversation with a man. One that wasn't simply him talking at her for two hours. She actually got to participate in this one.

And Billy wasn't just letting her talk to be nice, like Cliff occasionally did, barely waiting until she paused for a breath before butting in and taking the discussion back over.

Billy actually listened to her. Asked questions that proved it and kept her talking.

Like he really wanted to know her. What she thought.

Who she was.

Maryann wiggled her brows. "I'm sure I can come up with something."

She didn't have any intention of making him take her to the fanciest place around.

Because, thanks to him, she somehow managed to have the best night in as long as she could remember sitting in an uncomfortable seat, eating nachos and drinking beer.

"Good." Billy seemed a little happier thinking she was going along with his plan.

Maryann grinned at him as the announcer said something across the speaker.

Billy's eyes slowly lifted, looking toward the booth where the announcer sat. He checked his watch. "That took a lot longer than I expected."

Maryann moved to the edge of her seat, propelled there by excitement for the man at her side. "Is it time to announce the winners?"

"Almost." Billy tipped his head toward the booth at the edge of the private section where they were sitting. "But it looks like your date finally decided to figure out where you went."

Maryann turned to find Cliff standing at the base of the steps leading to the announcer's booth with two security guards. "Oh." She stood up, intending to head over to handle the situation. "I'll be right back."

Billy stood up right along with her. "I'm going with you."

"No." Maryann pressed one hand to the center of his chest as she passed him on her way to the end of the row of seats. "He needs to know this is *his* fault." She shook her head. "Not yours."

It was the truth. Even before Billy appeared, she hadn't intended to find her way back to Cliff's side. Not once it was clear he wasn't worried about finding his way to hers.

Billy's frown was deep and strong. "I don't want you going over there alone."

She smiled. "Too bad."

It was surprisingly easy to find her voice with Billy. Much easier than it had been with anyone else she'd spent time with.

And that included Cliff. She should have told him weeks ago that she wasn't interested in him, but the reasons she had didn't feel like they were good enough.

Because most of them sounded selfish and self-centered.

He didn't listen to her.

He didn't take her feelings or preferences into consideration.

He didn't care about her thoughts or opinions.

And he was just the last in a string of men who acted the same way, so she'd started to think that maybe she was asking too much.

But Billy proved her wrong.

And now it was time to give Cliff the truth. Hopefully he would take it to heart.

It was the final intermission before the winners were announced, so about half the people in attendance were taking their final trips to the bathroom and concessions, making her walk to the booth a little more congested than it would have been a few minutes ago.

By the time she made it to where Cliff was he'd started to pace, checking his watch every few seconds as the announcer called the five-minute warning for the awards presentation.

And she didn't want to miss it.

"Cliff."

He turned immediately, eyes going a little wide when he saw her. "There you are. I thought you left." He turned toward the grandstand. "Come on. If we hurry we should be able to make it back to our seats by the time they announce the winners."

He acted like it was completely normal for her to have been missing for hours. He didn't even look relieved that she was fine.

She'd intended to simply come tell him she wouldn't be accompanying him on any more of his weekend excursions, but now she was wondering what in the heck was going through his brain. "Where did you think I went?"

Cliff turned back to her, eyes staying on the arena. "I just figured you were off pouting somewhere."

So he knew she wouldn't like the rodeo? "Why didn't you bother trying to find me then?"

"I was trying to wait until you got over it, but obviously that wasn't happening before the end of the night." He finally looked at her. "So I figured I'd have to try to hunt you down."

"It's been hours." She wasn't shocked that Cliff didn't think of her happiness, but she was a little surprised that he didn't even consider her safety. "I could have been dead."

Cliff scoffed. "Don't be dramatic." He turned again. "Hurry up. I want to see who wins."

There it was again. Cliff worrying only about what he wanted. He didn't care where she'd been. Only that he got back to his seat in time to enjoy the last of the evening he planned for himself.

"I'm not going with you." Maryann stood a little taller, ready to do what she should have done before. "And I'm not interested in any more dates with you."

Cliff's brows lifted, reaching up toward the pristine cowboy hat on his head like he couldn't believe what he was hearing. "There's no reason to get all worked up about this. I'm not mad."

That's what he thought this was about? That she was concerned about his feelings? Worried that he was upset with her?

"At least one of us isn't." Maryann offered him the last smile he would ever get from her. "I hope you get everything you deserve in life."

It sounded snarkier than she intended. She genuinely did want the best for Cliff.

The best being that he would learn the world did not revolve around him.

She didn't wait for him to respond, there really wasn't any reason to. What he had to say didn't matter.

She had better, more interesting, things to get back to.

And it wouldn't take her long to get to them, considering Billy was standing three feet behind her, leaning against the chain-link fence keeping the attendees from getting too close to the dangerous situations they paid good money to witness.

No one would ever guess he was there for her. His attention was focused elsewhere. His tall frame was relaxed and casual, like he was simply another one of the people scattered around.

But she knew the truth.

And the truth had everything to do with why this night was turning out to be amazing.

She glanced at Billy as she strode past him, not saying a word as she walked away from Cliff, leaving him to stare after her.

And he was definitely staring.

She was probably the first woman who wasn't impressed by all the money he dished out.

But hopefully she wasn't the last. Hopefully Cliff figured out that even with all the money in the world, you should still try to give half a shit about the people around you.

Maryann made it back to her seat right as the announcer started through the awards.

"Did he really say what I think he said?" Billy was talking before he was even fully seated.

Maryann watched the center of the arena. "Probably, but it doesn't matter."

Not in the way Billy thought it did anyway.

Because she learned something important from Cliff and the words that came out of his mouth.

Something she should have figured out long before now.

Security didn't really come from money.

She wouldn't end up different from her mother just because she married a man who was more financially stable than her father managed to be. She would end up different from her mother if she married a man she could trust. A man who would always have her best interest at heart.

Because that's where true security came from. Two people who always had each other's backs.

CHAPTER SIX

"ARE YOU GLAD I made you stay?" Maryann looked mighty proud of herself and the fact that she'd managed to convince him not to leave the rodeo.

"I'm going to have to think about that one long and hard." He wasn't going to complain about getting to spend the evening next to her, but she would have had a lot more fun if they'd gone to the dinner she expected when her evening began.

"Are you saying you didn't have a nice time tonight?" Maryann wasn't trying to rope him into a confession. It was clear from the smile on her face she already knew that he had more than a nice time.

"What I'm saying is," Billy pulled out of the rodeo arena's lot, easing his truck onto the road, "that I'm pretty sure we could have had a much nicer time somewhere quiet and less crowded."

"But that's what you came all the way here for. It would've been crazy for you to leave." Maryann looked perfectly at home in the front seat of his truck, sipping on the foam cup of ice water he picked up for her on their way out.

Billy forced his eyes to the road even though all he wanted to do was keep staring at her beside him. "I'm not sure what I really came all the way here for."

He thought he knew, but was starting to wonder if maybe he'd been so caught up in the rodeo he didn't realize he'd outgrown it.

That it was past time for him to move on.

"Well, considering you've been working your way up to tonight for months, I think it's safe to say you came here to do exactly what you did." Maryann tapped one finger on the medal sitting in the console between them. "Win."

He didn't hate how proud she looked. She'd been the last one to stop clapping after his name was announced and he could hear her whistling from the stands as he went to claim his prize.

Normally, it would've been the highlight of the trip.

But the whole time he was standing there, all he could think about was getting back to the woman waiting in the stands.

"Winning isn't everything."

"Neither is money, but they're both something." Maryann didn't give him an inch, expertly putting him back in his place with a gentle reminder.

It was one of many things he'd noticed about her over the past six hours.

She wasn't pushy in an obvious way, but still managed to get her point across.

And he respected her for that. He'd been out with countless women who agreed with everything he said. Went along with whatever he wanted. Never disagreed. Never even had an opinion of their own.

And that got real old, real fast.

Maryann didn't hesitate to disagree with him or share her opinions, and she was sure as hell willing to put her foot down over exactly how they would be spending the evening.

She was strong and smart and obviously capable of handling whatever life threw at her.

Which made him wonder how she ended up at the rodeo in the first place.

It was one of the few things about her that made him pause. "Can I ask you a question?"

"Sure."

"Why would you go out with someone like Cliff?"

He'd seen very little of the man, which was a problem in and of itself. But what he had seen didn't cast the guy in a good light. And it was already clear that Maryann was smart as hell—smart enough that she would've seen Cliff for what he is.

Maryann let out a long sigh. "I've been thinking about that a lot tonight." She played with the straw of her cup, lifting it out of the plastic lid before pushing it back in. "I guess I always wanted someone stable, and I thought Cliff was."

"Someone different from your father."

She nodded. "Exactly. I don't want to go through the things my mother has had to go through." Her brows came together as she stared out into the night. "But I think I was confused about what stability really is."

"You thought that because Cliff had a good career and was smart with his money that he was a sensible choice." He didn't have to read between the lines too awful much to figure out what Maryann had been thinking. She was just looking for someone who checked off the boxes her father didn't.

The problem was, she was ignoring a whole hell of a lot of other boxes. Boxes he would argue might be even more important.

Like the one about a man not abandoning her at an event filled with thousands of people.

Maryann nodded. "I was trying to be smart. I thought it was better to make a decision with my head than with my heart."

"I'm not going to completely disagree with you." He'd been lucky enough to grow up with parents who were an excellent team. But they were much more than that. They were best friends, partners in crime, and loved the hell out of each other. Everything he wanted to find for himself. "But I think your heart's still gotta be in it."

It was what would get you through the tough times, because no matter how compatible two people were, there would always be tough times.

And that's where the heart mattered.

Maryann huffed out a little laugh. "That's probably

information I could have used four years ago when I was picking out my major."

"Not real excited about business management?" It was a little bit of a surprise because he could see Maryann doing well in that sort of environment.

Actually, he could see her thriving anywhere she chose to be.

She was smart. Determined. Kind. Thoughtful. If her work ethic was anything like the rest of her, he imagined she would be an asset wherever she landed.

But that didn't necessarily mean she would be happy there.

Maryann lifted a shoulder, letting it drop. "I should be. It was pretty easy to find a job that makes a decent amount of money."

"I feel like this goes back to the head and heart thing." It was what he'd been grappling with himself, only he went in the opposite direction Maryann did, chasing his heart across the country.

"I guess I just don't want to make a wrong decision."

"You're going to make wrong decisions in your life, there's no way around that." It was advice he should take himself. "But just because you make a wrong decision, doesn't mean you can't make another, righter one."

"I think that's easier said than done." Her eyes came his way and she gave him a little smile. "Especially since I just finished earning a four-year degree that cost me an arm and a leg."

"So figure out a way to use that degree how you want to." He didn't like the thought of Maryann limiting herself, especially when it was clear she had so much to offer. "You can still find a way to live the life you want."

Her gaze stayed on him as he merged onto the highway she instructed him to take. "What about you? Are you living the life you want?"

If someone asked him that question a week ago he would have answered it easily. Told them he was absolutely living the life he wanted.

But now...

Now he was more willing to admit that maybe it wasn't true.

That maybe the shine of bouncing from hotel to hotel and bronco to bronco, was starting to wear off.

That maybe staying in new city after new city was only making him miss the old town he thought he wanted to escape.

"I used to be, but I'm not so sure anymore." He'd never admitted his uncertainty to anyone.

And that included himself.

But he wanted to be honest with her. Maybe it was because Maryann was as far removed from the situation as it got—

Or maybe it was something else.

"Well that's unfortunate." Maryann's lips turned down at the edges, like she was more disappointed in his unhappiness than she was in her own.

Which wasn't acceptable.

"Seems like it's unfortunate for both of us." Billy glanced her way. "It's a shame that neither of us has been able to get our shit together."

He almost expected her to be upset at the insinuation.

Instead Maryann barked out a loud laugh. “It is sort of a shame, isn’t it?” She leaned back in her seat, closing her eyes. “Especially since I’m exactly where I planned to be.”

If that was true, then he was in the same boat she was. One that was docked exactly where he intended to put it. “You know what they say about the best laid plans.”

“So what does that mean for you? Will you be going home to Moss Creek, Montana to run your family’s ranch?” Maryann’s expression was blank, making it hard to tell what she thought about the possibility.

Hell, maybe she didn’t think anything of it. They’d only met each other hours ago. It would be stupid to think she gave a shit about how he spent the rest of his life.

But he couldn’t help but give a shit about how she spent the rest of hers.

“Probably.” Billy caught sight of the street she lived on. “What about you? You going to start your boring job Monday and keep on the path you planned?”

Maryann opened her eyes, brows coming together in thought. “I have to. I’ve got to pay my bills somehow.”

That was where they differed. Because while they might be in similar places in their lives, Billy had his plan B already laid out for him, all he had to do was pull the trigger.

Maryann didn’t have a plan B. She couldn’t go live

with her parents. She didn't seem to have a huge savings account to fall back on while she figured out what she wanted to do next.

She was stuck in the life she accidentally built.

And that irritated the shit out of him.

"Well if you ever need some time away to think about it, you're more than welcome to come visit me in Montana. We've got plenty of extra bedrooms." Inviting a woman he barely knew to follow him states away wasn't anything he would've ever seen himself doing.

But now that he'd done it, he couldn't stop thinking about showing Maryann around the sleepy little town he called home.

She would love the old buildings that lined Main Street. The peace and quiet of the fields. The stunning backdrop of the mountains.

Maryann rolled her head his way, giving him a sleepy smile. "I'll keep that in mind."

Billy slowly pulled into the driveway of the duplex she shared with her roommate Amanda. The porch light was on, along with a lamp on the other side of the large front window. "Looks like your friend is still awake."

Maryann huffed out a long breath. "Of course she is. She wants to hear how awful Cliff was tonight."

"I'm taking it she's not a fan of his?" He liked this Amanda woman without even meeting her.

"Not at all." Maryann slowly collected her purse and cup. "I probably should have listened to her."

"But then you wouldn't have met me." He was fishing, digging around for some sign that she was thinking the same crazy thing he was.

And it was definitely crazy.

"That's a good point." Maryann looped her purse over one shoulder. "Then I wouldn't have realized that the rodeo is more fun than I would have expected."

It wasn't quite what he was hoping for, but it was better than nothing.

She reached for the handle of her door.

"Hang tight." Billy jumped out of the truck. He wasn't quite ready to let her go, but he sure as hell wasn't going to let Maryann open her own damn door. Not after she spent the night in heels and a dress, sitting on a hard seat just so he could collect his winnings.

He glanced up at the front window of the house, the weight of eyes on his back making him even happier he'd gotten his ass out of the truck.

Maryann had her brows lifted at him as he opened the door. "I know how to get out of a truck."

"Good." He held out one hand. "That will probably come in handy tomorrow morning when I pick you up for breakfast."

"Breakfast?" She scoffed, but her smile was immediate. "I thought I was getting dinner?"

"You are." He'd spend every bit of what he won tonight if it meant more time with her. "Lunch too."

Maryann took his hand, holding it tight as she slid out of her seat. "It's like someone told you that I like to eat."

"Darlin', I just watched you single-handedly destroy

an entire tray of nachos and two shredded barbeque sandwiches. No one had to tell me anything." He'd been pleasantly surprised when she dug into their concession-stand dinner, eating enough that he wasn't worried she'd be going hungry anytime soon.

"I guess it's a good thing you won all that money then." She smiled up at him. "Because you're going to die when you see what I can do to an omelet."

CHAPTER SEVEN

"WHERE HAVE YOU been?" Amanda frowned at her from where she sat at the center of their hand-me-down couch, a bowl of popcorn on her lap and a two liter of Dr Pepper in her hand.

"What do you mean? I told you I wouldn't be home until after midnight." Maryann set her purse down on the table just inside the door, doing her best to look nonchalant.

"What I mean is, you look happy. You never look happy after you come home from a date with Cliff." Amanda shoved in a handful of popcorn and continued to talk. "Because he's a twat, and always manages to say something stupid." She swallowed down her mouthful. "Probably because he is stupid."

"He's not stupid." She wasn't defending Cliff, not really. Mostly she was defending her choice to let Cliff take her out so many times. "He's going to be an attorney."

"Intelligent and smart are two totally different things. You can be intelligent and still be an idiot." Amanda took a swig of her soda. "Not that I'm convinced he's either one of those."

"Then you'll be happy to know I won't be going out with him anymore." Maryann dropped down onto the couch beside her roommate and best friend, reaching in to steal some popcorn.

"Don't act like you kicked him to the curb for my benefit." Amanda's eyes slid her way. "Because you know damn well that I already peeked out into the driveway." A slow smile crept across her face. "And Cliff doesn't drive a big red pickup truck."

Maryann slumped down on the couch, letting her head drop back against the cushions. "I think I've lost my mind."

There was no thinking about it. She absolutely, unequivocally, had lost her mind.

Who met a man and thought the kind of things she was thinking after less than six hours together?

Nobody smart.

"Blue-eyed Cowboys will do that to you."

Maryann's head snapped toward her friend as her jaw went slack.

Amanda lifted her brows in mock offense. "What? Don't look at me like that." She turned back to the television in front of the window. "I just have really good vision."

"You do not." Maryann jumped up from the couch and started digging between the cushions. It didn't take her long to find what she was looking for. She yanked the item free and held it up between them. “Binoculars?”

Amanda lifted one shoulder. “You’re looking at what my Friday night consisted of. At least let me live vicariously through you.”

Maryann rolled her eyes, tossing the binoculars to one side as she plopped back down. “And whose fault is that? I know for a fact three different guys asked you out this week.”

Amanda was one of the most interesting people she’d ever met. She could carry on a conversation about literally anything, she was funny, and she was pretty as hell.

There was no shortage of men wanting to take her out.

“Meh.” Amanda seemed unimpressed. “None of them really interested me.”

“What does that mean?” Maryann snatched another handful of popcorn “None of them interested in you.”

“It means exactly what it sounds like it means.” Amanda said it like it should have been plain as day. “It means none of them interested me.”

“I’m going to need more clarification on that.” Maryann kicked off the heels she’d been stomping across the grass and gravel in before tucking her feet up under her butt. “Because I think I was being interested in the wrong things.”

“Oh, you absolutely were.” Amanda grinned. “And I have been impatiently awaiting the day you would realize it.”

“Don’t look so happy. I had to go on so many terrible

dates because of it." She'd been out with every boring man who asked her to dinner. They talked about themselves. They talked about the stock market. They talked about all their things and all their stuff.

None of them asked her about her life. Not one of them wondered about her dreams or plans for the future.

"You want a man who gives a shit about something besides himself." Amanda cringed a little as she dished out a painful possibility. "Otherwise you're just going to end up with someone like your father."

"That's not true. All the men I've gone out with have plenty more than two nickels to rub together." It was one of the primary criteria Maryann had. They had to be financially stable. Capable of paying their bills without running their bank accounts into the red.

"That's not how they're like your father." Amanda went back to digging through the bowl of popcorn. "They're like him in that they're all selfish. They only worry about what they want and what matters to them."

Maryann stopped chewing as her friend's words hit home.

"My dad isn't a bad person." The defense on him was a knee jerk reaction.

"Technically, neither is Cliff. He's not going to purposely hurt you. He wasn't trying to take advantage of you or lead you on. He genuinely did want to be with you." Amanda's lip curled. "But he only wanted to be with you on his own terms. He wanted a relationship that made *him* happy." She glanced Maryann's way. "But he couldn't care less about it making you happy."

Which was a lot like how her parents' relationship was.

Her father loved her mother and wanted to be with her. He wasn't mean or abusive, but his primary concern was whether or not he was happy in life. He knew her mother was stressed about their bills and debt. He just didn't care because he was getting what he wanted.

"How are you so smart?" Maryann dropped her head back against the couch, eyes fixed on her friend.

"I don't know, but I wish I could give a little bit of it back because it's turning out to be kind of a fun kill." Amanda tipped back some more soda. "Maybe I should let Cliff take me out on a boring date. At least I'd get some dinner."

"That's not necessarily true." Maryann yawned. "He didn't have any intention of taking me to dinner tonight." She dropped her feet to the floor and stood up. "And thinking about it is only making me more tired."

"Stop acting like you think you get to go to bed without telling me who brought you home." Amanda wiggled her eyebrows. "Because you are absolutely not falling asleep until I hear every last detail."

Unfortunately there were way too many details for Maryann to offer them all up to her friend, so she just had to give her the condensed version. "I think I met someone that I'm genuinely interested in."

Interested in didn't really seem adequate to explain the way she was feeling about Billy Pace.

Which was silly. They'd only known each other a

handful of hours at this point. There was no way she could feel anything other than general interest in him.

Yet she did.

"Really?" Amanda dragged the word out as she shifted around on the couch until she faced Maryann. "And what is it about this cowboy that is so magical?"

That was an answer she didn't want to offer up. Especially when it was as broad as it was.

Because everything about Billy Pace seemed magical at this point.

"Well, he won, for starters."

Amanda's brows came together. "Won what?"

"The rodeo. He won it." She was still just as impressed now as she was when they called Billy's name and he walked out into the arena. Men applauded, and more than a few women swooned.

Which she couldn't blame them for. Billy was definitely a swoon-worthy man.

Amanda's mouth dropped open. "Holy shit. You came home with the king of the rodeo?"

"Seems like I did." What he accomplished tonight was impressive as hell, but Billy's athletic abilities on a horse had little to do with why she was so fascinated by him.

"I guess that's one way to get into a woman's pants." Amanda lifted a brow at her. "You are going to let him in your pants, aren't you?"

"He didn't even try." Actually, Billy hadn't even attempted to kiss her.

Amanda shook her head. “Damn. I should’ve gone to the rodeo with you.”

“I guess it turns out Cliff had at least one good date idea.” Maryann almost choked on the giggle that the revelation brought on.

Amanda didn’t even try to contain hers. Her head dropped back as she cackled. “I bet it’s killing him that you left with another guy.” She smiled wide. “And I love it.”

“He doesn’t even know.” Maryann backed away from the couch. She wanted to get a good night’s sleep if she was going to be spending the whole day with Billy tomorrow. “I thought it was important that he realized I was not staying at the rodeo with him and it was all his own fault.”

“Savage. I love it.” Amanda grabbed the bowl of popcorn and stood up. “So when are you seeing this cowboy again?”

“Tomorrow.” Maryann couldn’t stop the smile that spread across her face. “He wants to take me out to a real dinner.”

“For once, I’m actually jealous of a date you’re going on.” Amanda carried her late-night snack into the small kitchen. “He doesn’t happen to have any cowboy friends, does he?”

“He does, but none of them are from around here.” Maryann snagged her discarded shoes before heading toward the hall leading to their bedrooms.

“Even better. A fun dinner, maybe a little ride around the cowboy, and then they ship out and go back to wherever they came from." Amanda flipped off the kitchen light before following her down the hall. "Sounds like a perfect scenario."

When you broke it down into its pieces, the situation might afford the opportunity for a little stringless fun and excitement, which was probably what many of the women at the rodeo watching Billy with adoring eyes were hoping for.

It's what *she* should be hoping for.

She didn't know Billy. It should be simple to think about having a little fun and then letting him go back home. To his ranch in Montana. To Moss Creek, the little town that sounded surprisingly interesting.

Amanda stopped just in front of her bedroom door, looking Maryann over with a wary gaze. "You got really quiet."

"I'm just tired, that's all." Maryann opened the door to her bedroom and stepped in.

"You really like this guy." Amanda grinned at her across the hall. "You like him a lot."

"We had a nice evening and a good conversation." That was it. Nothing more. "He probably just seems impressive because of who I went to the rodeo with."

"That is true. Cliff could make most men seem impressive." Amanda shook her head. "But that's not what this is, is it?"

She knew her best friend would be a problem. The second she saw the lights on inside the house, Maryann knew her friend would figure her out. "I barely know him." It was something she had to keep reminding herself of.

She barely knew Billy Pace. And even if she did get to know him better, he still lived in the middle of nowhere, Montana. Definitely not the kind of place she would easily be able to find a job that would ensure she would never end up like her mother.

"But you're going out with him again tomorrow." Amanda wiggled her brows. "To dinner." She backed into her room. "Which means we'll have plenty of time to discuss this before then."

"There's nothing to discuss." Maryann walked deeper into her room, blowing her friend a kiss good-night before closing the door.

She wasn't going to tell Amanda that they would not have plenty of time to discuss Billy Pace. Because Billy Pace made it clear he was coming to get her first thing in the morning, and feeding her not just dinner, but also breakfast and lunch.

Which meant she would have an entire day to figure out why he was definitely not a good match for her.

CHAPTER EIGHT

"YOU'RE TAKING HER out tomorrow?"

"Yup." Billy leaned back in his seat, kicking his boots off as he tipped back another drink of the beer his buddy brought over from the hotel room next door.

"You really think this is a good idea?" Justin stared at him. "It didn't look to me like she's the normal kind of woman that shows up to the rodeo."

"She's not." It was one of many things that had him trying to figure out ways to stay in town longer.

Most of the women who chased him around the rodeo weren't actually interested in him. They were more focused on what they believed he was.

"You can't take up with a woman who lives states away." Justin leaned against the small table tucked into the corner of Billy's hotel room. "Women like her don't wait on men like us, not while we travel around the country."

"Who said I expected her to wait on me?" This conversation was a long time coming, and now that it was here Billy couldn't wait to get it over with. "I'm done."

Justin's head bobbed back in surprise. "You're done?" He shook his head. "You can't be done. You're just getting started."

He wasn't technically just getting started. He was just finally getting where he wanted to be.

The top.

But it didn't give him what he thought it would. Not by a long shot.

"It's not all it's cracked up to be." The money was good. He'd made more in the past three months than he'd made in the last two years combined.

But like he told Maryann earlier, money wasn't everything.

"I think I'm going back to Moss Creek." It was the inevitability he'd been running from.

But now Billy was ready to turn around and face it head-on.

The possibility of spending the rest of his life in one place, doing one thing, didn't seem as unappealing as it once did.

Not when he started to consider the fact that he might not have to do it alone.

"And you think that girl is going to want to go home with you?" Justin shook his head. "She's got a whole life here. You've known her for what? Five minutes?"

"Six hours." He wasn't winning the argument his friend was making, but it didn't matter.

Because deep down he knew his friend was right.

The chances of Maryann deciding to up and leave her life here were slim to none, especially after only one day.

But tomorrow would make it two days, and maybe two days was enough.

"You need to sleep on this." Justin stood up, grabbing what remained of his beer as he pointed to Billy's bed. "Lay your ass down, and sleep whatever in the hell this is off. Tomorrow's a new day." His friend turned and opened the door. "Maybe by then you'll be more in your right mind."

Billy didn't have the heart to tell him that he felt in his right mind for the first time in a long time.

That he finally felt like he was starting to understand what life was all about.

What life *should* be all about.

He polished off his beer as he got ready for bed, showering off the dust of the day before turning in for the night.

Justin was right. Tomorrow was a new day.

But maybe it was more than that.

Maybe it was the start of a new life.

One he could see himself in for a long damn time.

"WELL, HELLO THERE." A red-headed woman grinned out at him as she leaned against the jam of the open door to Maryann's apartment. "You must be Billy."

"And you must be Amanda." He held out the first of the two flower bouquets he'd picked up on his way over.

Her brows lifted in surprise.

"It didn't seem right to bring flowers for one friend but not the other." He'd been raised right and wanted to be sure Maryann knew that.

But he also knew the best person to have on his side right now was the one standing in front of him.

Amanda wasn't just Maryann's roommate. Based on all the conversations they had last night, he knew she was also her closest friend.

"Wow." Amanda took the flowers, immediately leaning in to take a deep breath across the top of the arrangement.

The door yanked open wide as she was sniffing the roses, and Maryann looked from him to Amanda to the flowers in her hand.

"If you don't want to keep him then I do." Amanda shot him a quick grin as she backed away, making space for Maryann in the opening. "Thanks for the flowers, Bill."

"You're welcome." Because of Maryann he was ten-thousand dollars richer than he would have been, and he was happy to share the wealth.

Especially when it might help get him where he wanted to go.

And now that he'd laid eyes on her again it was clear

as day that he wanted to go wherever Maryann Morgan was headed.

"You look real nice." He passed over the second set of flowers. "These are yours." He leaned in. "I got you candy too, but we can keep that a secret."

"Damn it, Bill." Amanda hollered out from the small kitchen. "I was just starting to like you too." Her teasing tone was easy to discern as she went to work putting her flowers in a vase.

Maryann took a step back. "You can come in." She watched him closely as he came into the small living room at the front of the duplex.

"Am I what you remembered?" He was a little worried that he'd show up this morning and Maryann would have had time to think over the previous night, deciding that maybe a Montana cowboy wasn't anyone she wanted to spend her Saturday with.

Maryann lifted one shoulder. "I guess you'll do." Her lips curved in a small smile as she turned away, carrying her flowers into the kitchen. She opened a cabinet to reveal a line of vases before selecting a clear, cut-glass option with a wide mouth and pulling it free.

"That's quite a collection of vases you ladies have." Billy relaxed against the opening to the space and watched as they snipped stems.

"Amanda gets a lot of flowers from all the men who are trying to trick her into going out with them." Maryann peeked into the cabinet. "I think only one of those belongs to me."

"That's a shame." It was more than a shame. It was aggravating as hell.

Because it meant that chances were good, Cliff wasn't the first twat Maryann allowed to waste her time.

Maryann shrugged. "I didn't really see it that way." She was trying to brush off the slight. "Flowers die."

"It's not about the flowers." He was from the country. A tiny town in the middle of nowhere. He didn't go to college. Barely graduated high school.

And even he knew it wasn't about the fucking flowers.

It was about the thought behind them.

Amanda pointed at him. "Seems like you finally found a smart one."

Maryann's eyes opened wide as she turned toward her friend, shoving both the bouquet and the vase she selected in her roommate's direction. "Can you handle these for me?" She didn't wait for an answer before facing Billy, a tight smile frozen on her face. "Because I think we need to go."

"I only said it because it's true." Amanda pointed at Maryann's back as she mouthed her next words at Billy. "*She has terrible taste in men.*"

Amanda was trying to be a good friend. She clearly wanted Maryann to end up with someone who deserved her.

Her execution might leave a little bit to be desired, though.

"We do need to go." Billy rested one hand at the

center of Maryann's back, urging her toward the front door. "We've got a lot to do today."

He hadn't been able to sleep at all last night. He'd spent hours lying awake trying to think of a way to bring Maryann close enough she might consider seeing where this could go.

Because he absolutely wanted it to go somewhere.

It was crazy, not well thought out, and a little reckless.

Just like every other good decision he'd ever made in his life.

All he had to do was get Maryann on-board.

Billy opened the door and gave Amanda a nod as Maryann walked out in front of him. Amanda was as far on his side as she could be without knowing his true intentions, which he appreciated. Hopefully she'd planted a seed that he could help grow.

"It's a really nice day, isn't it?" Maryann looked much more casual this morning than she did last night. The dress and heels had been replaced by shorts, a t-shirt, and a pair of sandals. Her dark blond hair was pulled back in a ponytail and her face was scrubbed clean. She looked relaxed and maybe a little bit excited.

Hopefully he lived up to her expectations.

"It's a perfect day." Billy opened the passenger's door of his truck. "But I'm pretty sure we could've made any kind of day work."

That was part of why he knew it was such a good idea to be here today. With her.

Because every bit of him was positive they would

have fun no matter what. Rain or shine, cold or hot, it didn't matter.

Maryann rested one hand on his shoulder, using him for balance as she climbed up onto the running board. "I can imagine you find interesting things to occupy your time no matter what."

The assumption was flattering.

But he wasn't sure why she'd think that.

"What would make you say that?"

"Well, I watched you ride a horse that scrambled your brain, and I'm pretty sure you considered that a good time, so I figured the bar was pretty low." She grinned out at him from her seat in his pickup truck and the sight of her smiling face in that spot only sank his resolve deeper.

One way or another, he was going to figure out how to get more time with Maryann Morgan.

"Unfortunately, I'm also hoping that you'll have a nice time too, and I can't imagine you being too thrilled at the idea of losing any of your perfect brain cells on the back of a horse."

"Based on my lackluster dating history, I would say I probably can't afford to lose any of my brain cells on the back of a horse." Maryann didn't look as upset about the mention of her past dates today as she had the night before. If nothing else, hopefully that meant he was giving her the chance to consider better options.

Options like him.

Options like Moss Creek, Montana.

Options that might include life on a ranch and plenty of little girls that looked just like her.

And once again, he was getting ahead of himself.

It was how every train of thought he had last night ended.

With Maryann in Moss Creek, having his babies.

Which meant whether he wanted to claim it or not, he'd come up with an endgame.

All he had to do was work out how to get there.

CHAPTER NINE

"HAVE YOU EVER been here before?" Billy was close at her side as they made their way through the art museum.

She hated to tell him the truth. He'd clearly put so much time and effort into planning out this day. "I have. I actually come here all the time."

But Billy looked relieved at her response instead of disappointed in it. "Good."

Maryann turned toward him, studying his face instead of the priceless art hanging on the walls and positioned across the floors. "Why is that good?"

It was how most of this day had gone, her paying more attention to the man with her than all the things in front of them.

"Because it means I picked something you like to do." His smile was easy and soft. "This is your town, Darlin'. The chances of me picking something you've never done are slim to none."

"I've never been to the rodeo." She was trying to offer

up a unique experience they'd been able to share, thinking it would make Billy feel a little better about their time together.

And it clearly worked because his smile widened immediately. "And if it wasn't for Cliff, you still wouldn't have been to the rodeo, because it's something you didn't want to do." He turned his gaze to the portrait of a woman they'd been standing beside for almost five minutes. "I wasn't going to make the same mistake."

The fact that Billy spent so much time trying to think of things she would enjoy put a warmth in her belly.

A warmth that was immediately swallowed up by the pit that had been growing throughout the course of their day together.

"I liked the rodeo."

Billy lifted his brows at her.

"Mostly." She did enjoy the horses and many of the people. Even the food was surprisingly decent. "I didn't love watching you get your brain scrambled."

"That's pretty much the whole point of a rodeo." Billy's hand slid into hers as he led her toward the next painting. "For me, anyway." His blue eyes went to the large depiction of a man on the back of a rearing horse. "Looks like it is for him too."

"He's sitting up too straight." Maryann grinned when Billy's eyes snapped her way. "What? Just because I didn't love it, doesn't mean I wasn't paying attention." She turned back to the man riding the horse. This wasn't a painting she normally spent much time looking at, but now she couldn't help but notice it.

Not so much the man, but the horse.

It was beautiful. The animal exuded strength and power.

"Do you have an art museum in Moss Creek?"

Billy was quiet for a second and when his answer came it was short and clipped. "No."

Maryann's eyes found their way back to him, like they had so many times before. "That's a shame."

Billy nodded. "It really is."

They'd had a perfect day together. Seen many of the best things, in her opinion, that San Jose had to offer.

Eaten great food. Enjoyed easy conversation.

It was the most wonderful, terrible day she'd ever had.

Because at the end of all of this, Billy would be leaving.

The rodeo was over today and all the friends he traveled with would be packing up and shipping out, moving on to their next destination.

And taking Billy along with them.

Billy's hand stayed tight around hers as they moved through the next few exhibits silently, quietly passing the first wordless minutes they'd had all day.

Everything had come so easily, in spite of the fact that they'd been together nearly eight hours straight.

But the closer they got to the end, the more difficult it became.

Because she didn't really want it to end.

She didn't want Billy to leave and go back to Moss Creek.

She didn't want her life to go back to what it was before he offered his help less than twenty-four hours ago.

And the weight of that realization was weighing on her more and more with each passing minute.

Because Billy would be going back to Moss Creek, and her life would be going back to normal.

Whatever that meant.

They stopped at the last painting, each staring at it silently. It was a beautiful landscape. Rolling pastures. Wood fencing. Grass that almost seemed to be moving in a soft breeze and mountains that appeared to hold every color of the rainbow.

It was the most beautiful place she could imagine. Nothing like the cityscape she woke up to and existed in every day.

"That could be a painting of my ranch." Billy's eyes lingered on the painting a second longer before slowly moving her way. "Except it's missing cows."

She wasn't really well-versed on what all was involved in running a ranch. "You raise cattle?"

Billy tipped his head in a nod as he turned back to the painting. "Yeah. Lots of them."

"Do you like working on the ranch?" She knew Billy chased his rodeo dreams across the country, and initially she assumed that meant he didn't enjoy his life on the ranch, but the way he was looking at the painting made her reconsider that assumption.

Billy took a deep breath and slowly let it back out. "I do. I think I missed it more than I realized I did."

"If Moss Creek looks anything like this, I can see how that would happen." She was from a little town stuck between two big cities. There were no mountains. No grassy fields. Not even a lake or stream to cut through the man-made landscape.

And she didn't miss it. Not for a single second.

But if it had looked like this painting in front of them, she might never have left.

"I can't imagine what it would be like to grow up someplace like that." If she'd learned one thing from all the conversations they had last night and today, it was that Billy's life was vastly different from her own.

His parents were still happy and in love, working together to run the ranch. They'd gone many years without being able to have children, and he was a late-in-life surprise they embraced wholeheartedly. He was loved, appreciated, and encouraged to spread his wings and fly.

Even when they were more than ready to retire, his parents still didn't pressure him to rush back home and take his spot as the head of Red Cedar Ranch.

She had also been a surprise. One her parents frequently referred to as *the accident*.

Her father never wanted children, probably because he was smart enough to realize he was too selfish to be a good parent.

He didn't want to share his money. He didn't want to share her mother.

That frequently left Maryann at the bottom of the

barrel when it came to having her needs met, emotional or otherwise.

No one really supported her. No one was eagerly awaiting her return.

She was essentially on her own. Always had been.

"You really should come see it sometime. I think you'd love it." Billy's words were soft. Almost hesitant.

Like he wasn't quite sure if he really wanted her to come or not.

"I would like that a lot." She would travel to Moss Creek in a heartbeat if he asked her.

Hell, she might pack her bags tonight if the offer was made.

But Billy didn't make the offer. Instead, he led her out of the museum and back into his truck, loading her up before pulling away to their last stop.

The dinner he was so sure she needed.

But right now, sitting in a restaurant, acting like everything was fine, didn't sound like how she wanted to spend her final hours with the man who opened her up to a whole new way of thinking.

One she was ashamed hadn't occurred to her before.

"What if we skip dinner?" Maryann kept her eyes straight ahead, not really sure she wanted to look at him and gauge his reaction.

Because she was starting to think maybe she was reading too much into this.

Making it more than it really was.

"And do what instead?" Billy's tone didn't hint at

what he was thinking, and it forced her to decide between soldiering on or taking it back.

But she'd spent too much time letting men dictate her evenings. What she did. Where she went.

And it was time for that to stop.

"What if we go back to my apartment?" She struggled to take a tiny breath. "Maybe order pizza?"

"Pizza?" Billy glanced at her across the cab of his truck. "You want to eat pizza for dinner?"

She did, actually. "You don't like pizza?"

"I love pizza." He turned back to face the road, his mouth pressed to a thin line. "It's just not a very impressive dinner."

"Maybe I don't need an impressive dinner." She didn't want Billy to think she was something she wasn't. "I don't actually care about things like that."

"I know that."

He said it so quickly it made her pause. "You do?"

"Of course I do." He turned, his blue eyes holding hers. "Just because you don't care about it, doesn't mean I still don't want to give it to you."

Gosh darn it.

She was working hard to keep her head with this man and he undermined her ability at almost every turn.

Which only made her more certain she wanted to spend their last hours together somewhere quiet.

Somewhere he could be only hers.

"But if you really want pizza—"

"I do." She didn't bother trying to seem casual about

it. What was the point? Their time was running out so she didn't have anything to lose.

Except maybe the first man who listened to her. Thought about her wants and interests.

Billy hooked one hand over the top of the wheel as he turned back toward her apartment. "I guess pizza it is then."

The driveway was empty when they pulled up in front of the duplex she and Amanda shared with a sweet older couple who liked to bring them cookies. It was the first place she loved living and Maryann assumed that was because it was hers.

But maybe that had more to do with Mr. And Mrs. Kinley and Amanda.

Maybe it was because she was surrounded by people who genuinely cared about her for the first time in her life.

"Do you have neighbors in Moss Creek?"

"Neighbors?" Billy slowly smiled. "None that you can get to without a decent drive."

"That's sad." But at least it dimmed her growing interest in Moss Creek, Montana. "I can't imagine not having someone to check in on or wave at every day."

Billy's smile grew as he faced her. "You've never lived in a small town, have you?"

Maryann shook her head. "No. Why?"

"Cause there's plenty of people checking in on each other." He opened his door. "Only we call it bein' nosy." His door closed, forcing her to bank her response as Billy made his way around the truck.

The second he opened her door she set it free. “Maybe they’re not being nosy. Maybe they just genuinely want to make sure the people around them are okay.”

Billy’s brows barely pinched together as his eyes moved over her face. “I like the way you look at the world, Maryann Morgan.” He reached in, grabbing her around the waist and hauling her free of the truck. “Even if you won’t let me take you to that fancy dinner I promised you.”

CHAPTER TEN

JUST WHEN HE thought Maryann couldn't get any more perfect, she went and threw him for another loop.

He'd spent the whole day proving that he paid attention when she talked. Doing everything possible to make it clear that even after just a few hours, he knew her well enough to plan a day she would love.

And then she turned it all on its head and decided to end it with an evening he would love.

Which was getting her—mostly—to himself.

He might have to share her with Amanda, but even that would offer him insight he needed.

Needed because his time was running out.

And while Maryann did seem to appreciate the painting that reminded him of home, she certainly wasn't chomping at the bit to come home with him.

He'd even tried mentioning her visiting again, thinking maybe she would agree and they might be able to get a date on the book.

But she didn't.

Which meant he still had work to do.

"How do you feel about beer?" Maryann stayed right at his side as they walked up the steps to the little duplex.

"I might call myself a connoisseur." He shot her a grin. "I might also call myself a connoisseur of pizza."

Maryann's smile was wide and immediate. "Then I think I know of a place you are going to love." She fished her keys from her purse and shoved one into the deadbolt, twisting it open.

The girls lived in a nice neighborhood, but it made him feel better to know that they kept the door locked. Especially considering he was about to head thousands of miles away.

Maryann went straight inside, setting her purse on the table just inside the door as she walked toward the kitchen and grabbed the phone from the wall. "There's a place right down the street that makes the absolute best pizza." She punched the number in without having to look it up, which meant she ordered from there often enough to have it memorized.

And often enough to make him think he wouldn't be the only one to enjoy their altered dinner plans.

"Their crust is so good." Maryann was still going on about the pizza as she waited for the line to start ringing. "I don't know how they bake it, but somehow it ends up almost crispy around the edges." Her eyes moved to one side as she curved the phone under her mouth. "Hey. It's Maryann."

The pizza place was on a first name basis with her.

If he hadn't been positive this was a woman he could fall in love with before, he absolutely was now.

"No, I think I'm going to order something different today." She tapped her fingers on the counter. "How about a medium Mediterranean and a medium cowboy supreme." She wiggled her brows at him, clearly proud that she knew a place with a namesake pizza.

"Oh." She stood a little straighter. "And can you send me a six-pack of Heineken?" She was quiet for a second, probably as they read her order back to her. "Perfect. Thank you." She hung up and let out a breath as she turned his way. "You want to watch a movie?"

Billy glanced down the hallway. "Should we ask Amanda if she wants to watch a movie with us?" A woman's friends were important, and he was pretty sure Amanda would be a key piece in getting Maryann to visit Montana.

Hell, Amanda could come with her if that's what it took to get her there.

"Amanda's not here." Maryann's snagged a couple of sodas from the fridge before coming into the living room. "She went home to visit her parents this morning. She'll be gone until tomorrow night." She held out one of the drinks. "It's just you and me."

It was what he wanted.

To have Maryann to himself.

But now that it was here, Billy was doubting how great of an idea it really was.

Because he wasn't confident in his own ability to make smart choices.

Ones that wouldn't haunt him for the rest of his life.

And he could see how getting too close to Maryann Morgan and losing her forever could haunt a man.

Cliff was probably already feeling the regret. Second-guessing every terrible decision he made.

"What's wrong?" Maryann settled onto the couch beside him, her body close enough that the bad decisions were already starting to creep in.

Surely kissing her wouldn't be enough to cause a problem.

Maybe a little touching.

But that would have to be all.

At least until she decided to come to Moss Creek.

Then he would pull out every trick he had to get her to stay.

"Nothing." Billy shifted a little in his seat, trying to look more comfortable than he felt. "You lived here long?"

"About four years." Maryann sipped from her soda before leaning toward the coffee table to set it on a coaster.

When she leaned back, her side was almost pressed against his. "Amanda posted in the school newspaper that she was looking for a roommate and we got along immediately." Maryann tucked her feet up under her behind as she rocked even closer. "Which was fantastic because then I didn't have to figure out how to pay to live on campus."

"That's good." He was trying hard to follow the conversation, but the closer she got, the harder it was to focus on anything but the fact that he wanted to pull her against him.

Hold her close.

Not because he wanted anything more, though it was becoming clear he wouldn't pass that up, but because it was what felt right.

"What about you?" Maryann leaned into his side, stealing any room remaining between them. "Where does a cowboy hang his hat at night?"

"I guess that depends on the cowboy." He knew more than a few that spent each night in a different bed, taking full advantage of the opportunities their profession offered.

Maryann's lips quirked. "I would imagine the options are pretty unlimited, based on how many women I saw looking your way."

She wasn't wrong, but he didn't want Maryann thinking he was out chasing more than just the freedom he thought he wanted. "I'm not so interested in my options."

Maryann's eyes moved over his face, like she was looking for something. "I wouldn't blame you if you were." Her lips twisted in a smirk that dragged his attention to her mouth. "If handsome men were lining up for my attention my nights might have been more interesting than they were."

He couldn't stop the lift of his brows. "Really?"

Maryann returned his lifted brow expression. "Does that surprise you?"

Surprise wasn't the right word for how he was feeling.

Terror was a better option.

He was hoping Maryann might be a little more reserved when it came to physical closeness and all that could come with it.

If she wasn't then his evening was about to get a hell of a lot more difficult.

And a hell of a lot more risky.

"How about that movie?" He didn't wait for her answer before standing up and going to switch the set on. It was a pretty nice model with a screen that had to be at least twenty inches across.

Maryann's lips pursed, eyes sharp as she watched him work through the channels. He finally settled on something that looked to be a movie and went back to the couch, sitting a few inches from the woman who might test his willpower more than anyone else ever had.

She cleared her throat, smoothing her hair behind one ear as he pretended to focus on the movie, saying a silent prayer that she wouldn't reclaim the gap he'd put between them.

It was a marked difference from how most of their time together had gone, but for the first time he felt uncomfortable.

And it had everything to do with how easily he could get very comfortable with the woman beside him.

The more time he spent with her the more he realized he was already in way over his head.

It was a feeling he wasn't used to and didn't know how to manage.

He'd spent years chasing a challenge, stalking it from rodeo to rodeo, searching for the thing that would bring him the challenge he needed.

Because running Red Cedar Ranch certainly wasn't going to cut it.

But maybe he'd been going about it all wrong.

A knock at the door offered him a reprieve from the temptation he knew could easily get the better of him.

He jumped up, beating Maryann to the door as he pulled out his wallet and paid for the pizza and beer their delivery driver passed over.

Billy brought their food back to the coffee table, flipping open the cardboard lid and lining the pizzas down the center before setting out two bottles of Heineken and taking the rest to the fridge. By the time he got back Maryann was already halfway through her first slice, feet kicked up on the coffee table as she watched the movie and sipped her beer.

He hadn't spent a Saturday like this in a long time, but it was easy to imagine this being his new normal.

Only not in California.

Billy settled in on the couch and grabbed a slice from the same box Maryann took hers from.

She watched as he took the first bite. "What do you think?"

"It's good." He swallowed the rest of what was in his mouth. "Real good."

"That's the cowboy one." She took another bite of her own slice.

"And what do you think of it?"

She swallowed what was in her mouth, licking her lips in a motion that was almost painful for him to witness. "It turns out you're not the only cowboy I like."

They settled into an easy silence, eating their food, drinking their beers, and staring at the television in front of them.

Not that he could tell you a thing about what they were watching.

He was having a hard time focusing on anything but the woman sitting beside him.

When they were finished, Maryann packed the left-overs into one box, condensing them down before sliding them into the refrigerator. She dropped back beside him just as the credits rolled across the television screen. "What did you think of the movie?"

He thought about lying. Considered telling her the movie was great.

But that's not how he wanted to start out with her.

"I couldn't tell you a thing about that movie." He held her gaze, unable to look away. "I can't seem to do anything but look at you."

She lifted one brow at him. "Is that so?"

Billy tipped his head in a slow nod. "Unfortunately, it is."

Maryann's other brow jumped up to match the first. "Unfortunately?"

"Seems like I'll have to come up with another pastime since I'm supposed to head out tomorrow morning." He let the statement hang in the air, hoping she might ask him to stay.

Offer to go with him.

Make plans to see him again.

Something.

But instead she just gave him a small smile. "I'm sure you'll find something to occupy you."

He had.

But getting her where he wanted her was proving to be more of a challenge than he expected.

Maryann reached out to pick a bit of crusty pepperoni off his shirt. "Hopefully you enjoyed your time in California."

Billy caught her hand as she started to pull it away, holding it tight in his as he tried to find the right words.

But words had never been his strong suit.

Maryann's gaze held his, her lips barely parted as the seconds ticked by, each one stealing a little more of his sanity.

Of his sense.

Until he was left with nothing but need and longing to guide him.

Which was a dangerous combination.

One that pulled his hands to her face, curving around it as he leaned in to take her mouth with his.

CHAPTER ELEVEN

KISSING BILLY PACE might be the best, worst idea she'd ever had.

Not that it was entirely her idea.

If it had been entirely her idea, she would have kissed him before the pizza came.

And right now she was regretting that wasn't what happened.

Because, like everything else he did, Billy Pace put his whole heart into where his lips met hers.

It was a characteristic she was starting to realize permeated so deep it might be the essence of who he was.

And the thought of that was a little intoxicating.

Intoxicating enough that she couldn't wait to see what else Billy would put his whole heart into.

She wasn't a virgin, but her experience with men in the bedroom was a whole lot like her experience with them outside of it.

Lackluster and very one-sided.

She hadn't known Billy long, but in that small amount of time it was already obvious that any time she spent with him would be more about her than it was about him.

And that was a temptation she might not be able to resist.

Billy's hands slid from her face into her hair, sliding down the strands as his lips worked along her jaw and down her neck in tiny nips that sent goosebumps across her skin and pulled her nipples tight.

"You taste as good as you smell." His voice was a low rumble as he continued to drag his mouth lower, following the v-cut neckline of her t-shirt. One finger hooked into the fabric before his blue eyes lifted to meet hers. "Can I keep tasting you, Miss Maryann?"

She'd be an idiot to tell him no.

And she was a lot of things, but an idiot wasn't one of them.

"Yes." her voice was breathless and barely audible as she fought to keep enough air in her lungs.

"If you change your mind, just let me know." He pulled down, dragging both her shirt and her bra to one side, exposing her breast.

She arched her back, expecting him to make good on his offer, but Billy made no move to pull her nipple into his mouth.

Instead he reached out to run the tip of one finger around it, circling the puckered tip with a torturous touch. "Just as pretty as the rest of you."

She wiggled, trying to get a little closer to him, hoping to remind him of the permission she granted.

"Somethin' wrong, Darlin'?" There was a teasing edge in his tone.

Like he knew how frustrating he was being.

And was enjoying it.

"You know what's wrong." She couldn't say it.

Couldn't bring herself to ask for what she desperately wanted.

So she was at his mercy. Forced to take what he offered.

Thankfully the man seemed ready to offer a lot.

"I figured you'd be impatient." Billy curved his hand under the weight of her breast, lifting it to his mouth. She gasped as his lips latched around her, the deep pulling suck shooting straight to her pussy, creating an ache that built with each rake of his teeth and flick of his tongue.

“I’m not impatient.” She was very patient.

She’d spent four years waiting for a man who saw her.

Listened to her.

Treated her like she mattered.

Billy was all those things and more.

And she didn’t want to wait anymore.

Billy’s lips curved to a smile as they worked their way back up her body to press against hers. “I hope you’re a little impatient.” He tugged her closer, pulling her body in until her thighs straddled his. “Because I’m feeling a little impatient myself.” He wrapped one arm around her, holding tight to her waist as he pushed to his feet. “And a little like I need more room.”

Maryann yelped a little as she was hauled into the air, wrapped around a cowboy with more strength than any of the men she’d wasted her time on up to this point.

Combined.

“You got any problem with me takin’ you to your bedroom?”

The question was one more thing that set Billy apart from the men she’d known before.

Considering her legs were around his waist and her mouth was plastered to his, it was pretty obvious she was on board with everything that was happening.

But he asked anyway.

“Only if you drop me on the way there.” She clenched her thighs a little tighter, just in case her weight was starting to add up.

“I promise not to drop you, Miss Maryann.” Billy’s blue eyes stayed on hers as he moved them down the hall. “Not ever.”

The way he said it made her belly clench with a warmth that had nothing to do with the heat between her legs. “Okay.”

He paused in front of the laundry closet, looking between the two bedrooms at the end of the hall. “Where are we headed?”

She pointed to the one on the left before tucking her arms in as he angled them sideways, navigating the doorway to her room before tumbling down across the blankets covering her bed.

It was the sexiest thing that had ever happened to her.

Not that there was much competition in that department.

Billy crawled over her, his wide body blanketing hers as the seriousness of the moment started to sink in.

The men who'd been there before landed in her bed because it was the way things worked. Relationships had a certain progression they followed, and she adhered to those standards.

It was fine.

But bringing this man into her bed went against all of that.

Billy hadn't taken her out on multiple dates.

He hadn't talked to her on the phone.

He didn't slowly work his way up to this level of physical intimacy, moving through the stages of petting and kissing and touching until there was nowhere else to go but penetration.

Billy skipped all of it.

And was still moving too slow for her.

Maryann grabbed at his t-shirt, yanking it free from the waistband of his jeans, wrestling it up the lean line of his muscular body until it got trapped under his arms.

So she yanked harder, fighting the fabric.

Billy chuckled low and deep as he pushed to his knees. "Definitely impatient." He reached behind his head, gripping the back of his shirt and tugging it up and over his head, each move flexing the tight line of muscles that covered every inch of his body.

All the air rushed from her lungs, taking two words with it. "Holy shit."

How was it possible for a man to look the way he did?

She reached out to drag her fingers over his stomach, just to make sure it was real.

Just to make sure he was real.

Because so far Billy Pace was seeming like he might be too good to be true.

"I'll take that." He smirked at her blatant perusal of his body as he eased down over her again. His hands and mouth picked up where he left off, slowly peeling away each article of her clothing until she was completely naked and half out of her mind.

Or maybe she'd entirely lost her mind, because at this point if Billy asked her to pack up and go to Moss Creek with him, she just might do it.

Which was the craziest thing she could imagine anyone doing.

Billy's blue eyes raked down her naked body, the slow sweep so heavy it almost felt like a touch. "You're the prettiest thing I've ever been lucky enough to have my hands on."

"Thank you." She didn't know what else to say. Couldn't have come up with anything better if she tried, because one of Billy's big, rough hands started to follow the same path as his gaze, sliding down the center of her belly, making a path right to her—

She sucked in a sharp breath as his fingers skimmed between her thighs, the touch teasingly light as he traced the seam of her pussy. "Of course I'd be happy to stop touching you if that's what you want."

"Don't you dare." She grabbed his arm, holding it just in case he decided to make good on the threat.

"It's good to know we're feelin' the same way." His probing fingers pressed deeper, sliding against her slick flesh as he narrowed the scope of his touch to one specific area. "Because I'd sure be disappointed to find out you aren't enjoying yourself right now." His thumb settled onto her clit as one finger slid into her body, curving into her at an angle that stole any rational thought she still possessed.

It was impossible to do more than breathe, and even that was pushing it.

At this point she'd normally be doing her best to look like she was enjoying herself and the lackluster performance the man she was with offered.

That wasn't an issue she currently had.

Especially not when Billy's large frame shifted, wide shoulders wedging between her legs, as his mouth latched onto her clit, the steady flick of his tongue threatening to send her over the edge faster than she'd ever experienced.

Her thighs clenched tight, the move involuntary and unstoppable.

"Not yet, Darlin'." Billy gripped her knees, holding them tight as he raised his mouth from her aching mound. "I'm not done with you."

She made a foreign sound. One that was almost feral and definitely frustrated.

But Billy didn't seem affected by her obvious fury as he wedged his legs between hers, keeping them spread as he dug into his pocket and pulled out a strip of condoms, dropping them to the mattress.

Maryann did a quick count. "Why'd you bring five?"

"Cowboys are like Boy Scouts. We're always prepared." Billy worked the buckle of his belt loose. "And have you seen yourself?" He unzipped his fly and pulled out the straining line of his cock, fisting one large hand around it as his eyes moved over her body, spread wide and at his mercy. "You should be glad I didn't bring ten."

She swallowed hard as he reached for the strip and tore the first one off, ripping the foil pack open before rolling the rubber into place. Her heart beat faster with each passing second until she was worried about her own ability to survive the night.

Billy leaned in, one hand pressing into the pillow next to her head as his lips brushed hers. "Somethin' wrong?"

She managed to shake her head, swallowing down a whimper as he slid the head of his sheathed cock up and down her slit. "I'm fine."

Billy notched against her. "Maybe we can change that."

Penetration usually felt like an invasion. One she was fine with, but didn't necessarily crave.

But the slow press of his body was more like the filling of a void.

The completion of something she didn't realize was unfinished.

"Ohh." The air rushed from her lungs as he seated himself, stretching her in ways that weren't only physical.

Billy pulled back, the movement slow and steady, before easing back in, his eyes on her face, watching as his body once again met hers.

It was so much more than usual, and significantly more pleasant, but not the earth-shattering type of scenario the movies made it out to be.

"Hmm." Billy hooked one hand behind her knee, bending her leg up and out to the side as he leaned closer.

Then he thrust into her again.

The slight change in position opened her wider. Wide enough that his body could drag against hers as he moved, putting pressure and friction right where she needed it.

The sensation was shocking enough to make her yelp in surprise, fingers digging into his shoulders as she reacted.

"That's better." Billy's lips were still in a satisfied smirk when they took hers, claiming them as expertly as he was claiming the rest of her.

Better was right.

Each move he made hit places she didn't know existed, sending her racing toward a climax she wasn't prepared for.

Her body buckled, muscles and lungs seizing as she made sounds she should be ashamed of.

Sounds she might have to apologize for later.

Except Billy didn't seem to mind.

If anything, he seemed to be having some struggles of his own as his movements lost their rhythm and his jaw clenched tight.

A second later he groaned out a questionable sound of his own, fists gripping the pillow behind her head tight as he buried himself into her body and went still, breath raspy and rough. "Shit." He dropped his head to rest against hers. "That was supposed to last a lot longer."

Maryann tried to flatten down the smile his admission brought on, but it was impossible. "I guess it's extra good you brought more than one condom then."

CHAPTER TWELVE

"DIDN'T EXPECT TO see Billy Pace sittin' here at the bar tonight." Clint eased down onto the stool beside him, reaching one hand out for a shake. "When did you get back in town?"

Billy gripped his high-school buddy's hand tight, hoping it might steady the swimming in his head that was only half caused by the glass of whiskey in front of him. "Week ago."

Clint leaned back in his seat as he spun to face the bar. "How long you stayin'?"

It was a completely normal question. One his old friend had probably asked him a hundred times over the years.

Because up until now, he was always planning to leave.

Billy picked up his glass and tipped back what was left inside, sending it to the same place he'd sent the previous four glasses. "A while I guess."

Clint chuckled. "I know what your version of a while is." He lifted one finger when the bartender looked his way. "So that means your ass will be gone by the weekend."

The bartender dropped off Clint's beer, pausing to look down at the empty glass in front of Billy. "You want another one?"

"Yup." He'd done his damnedest to work off the foul mood that followed him home, spending most of the week busting his ass around the ranch, helping his dad catch up on repairs and maintenance.

It was an unsuccessful venture, but at least the ranch looked a hell of a lot better.

So now he was here, sitting at the bar with a new plan to drink away any memory of the reason he was back in Moss Creek.

Alone.

When Maryann kissed him goodbye and sent him on his way, without so much as a mention of seeing each other again, he'd done the only thing he could. He packed up his shit and drove through the night, heading back to the only place he wanted to be.

Home.

But that desire was turning out to be short-lived, because, in reality, the only place he actually wanted to be was with her.

Clint drank down some of his beer, watching Billy from the corner of his eye.

It was only a matter of time before the ranch hand

started throwing out questions Billy didn't really feel like answering.

Hopefully his next drink would arrive before that happened.

Unfortunately, that would also mean there was no telling what might come out of his mouth.

Probably the truth.

Clint stayed silent even after Billy's next whiskey arrived, eyes focused on the screen of the television set on the counter behind the bar. His friend was acting like it was a normal night.

It wasn't.

And Billy couldn't make himself pretend like it was.

"I met a woman." Billy stared down into his glass before swallowing more of the liquid that was supposed to get him through this night.

"Figured." Clint glanced his way. "You got that look of misery about you."

Misery didn't feel like an awful enough word to describe the way he was feeling.

Clint's eyes went back to the television. "You meet her at the rodeo?"

Billy tipped his head in a nod. "She came there on a date."

Clint grinned. "She leave with you?"

Billy nodded again. "Yup."

Clint turned his stool away from the TV to focus on where Billy sat. "How'd her city boy take that?"

"Don't know." Billy downed the rest of his whiskey,

grimacing at the burn as it worked its way to his stomach. “Don’t care.”

“Fair enough.” Clint looked him up and down. “Where’s this lady of yours now?”

“Don’t know.” He left it at that because in this instance he did care.

That was most of what landed his ass in the seat it was in.

Clint stared at him for a few long seconds before turning back to the television. “She not as interested in being a cowgirl as you thought?”

“Guess not.” He thought for sure Maryann would want to make some concrete plans with him to come to Moss Creek. Spend a little time in the town he called home.

He’d hinted that she should come more than once. Done everything he could think of to make it clear he wanted what they had to become more.

He thought she felt the same way he did. Thought she believed they had a future outside of that one weekend too.

Discovering he was the only one thinking that hurt more than it should have, and made him realize his life on the road was over.

He'd never be able to sit at another rodeo without thinking of her. Without looking for her in the crowd.

Without hoping she'd had a change of heart and came to find him the way he wanted to go find her.

Clint looked him over. "What did she say when you asked her to come here?"

Billy huffed out a bitter chuckle. Clint had never left Moss Creek and obviously didn't realize how things like this worked. "You don't just ask a woman you met two days ago to move to your hometown."

Clint stared at him for a few long seconds. "Are you telling me you didn't actually ask her to come here?"

Billy leaned back, the movement almost tipping him over. "Of course not. I'm not going to put her on the spot like th—"

Clint held up one hand, putting a stop to Billy's explanation. "So you didn't specifically ask her to move here." He lifted his brows. "Did you specifically ask her to visit?"

Billy barked out a bitter laugh. "Of course. I told her she could come here."

He came into the bar frustrated, thinking the buzz of alcohol might ease that, but Clint's line of questioning was only making everything worse.

"You told her she could come here?" Clint shook his head. "No woman in her right mind is gonna take that as an invitation."

Billy threw his hands out at his sides. "Why wouldn't she? I brought it up a few times. Told her she should come check the place out sometime."

Clint shook his head. "I thought you were smarter than this, Bill." He turned back to the game playing across the screen. "No woman in her right mind is gonna come to a little town in nowhere Montana for a man who won't even nut up and tell her he wants her here."

Billy scoffed, staring at the side of his friend's head.

Clint was wrong. Had to be.

He'd made it clear as hell to Maryann that he wanted to see what they could have.

Hell, he already knew what they could have. The second he laid eyes on her—standing in the middle of that dirty field, lookin' at home and out of place at the same time—he knew she was what he'd been looking for.

Maryann's world was completely different from his, but she still easily found her footing and fit right in.

But telling her all that would have been foolish. Too much, too fast.

Right?

"So you're saying I should have told her I wanted to marry her and she would have jumped right in my truck and come back here?" He laid out Clint's plan, expecting it to sound just as dumb out loud as it did in his head.

But hearing the words only drove home just how true they might be.

Clint slowly turned back his way, looking Billy up and down. "Do you want to marry this woman?"

There's no way he could. He barely knew Maryann and she barely knew him. They'd spent less than a holiday weekend together. No one could kno—

"Hell yes." The admission lifted a weight from his shoulders. One he didn't realize was dragging him down. "If she walked in this bar right now I would happily haul her ass to the courthouse and marry her today."

It might be stupid. It might be naïve.

But it also might be right. And that was the one he should have gone with.

Clint’s brows slowly lifted. "Seems like you've got some work to do then." He refocused on the game, tipping back his beer. "Figure out how to get out of that hole you're in, cause I’m guessin’ it’s pretty damn deep."

Billy waited, hoping Clint might offer up a little more advice, but his friend went silent again.

"How do I do that?" He'd spent years being at the top of his game. Going from town to town proving he was the best at what he did. Struggling wasn't something that came naturally to him. It wasn't a great feeling.

"There’s a few options, I guess." Clint tipped his head to one side, like he was mulling them over. "You could send her flowers."

Billy was shaking his head before Clint finished talking. "No flowers." He'd seen the vases lined through that damn kitchen, and even if Maryann claimed most of them were her roommates, he knew damn well at least a few were hers. "Flowers won't impress this woman."

Clint turned to face him, once again abandoning the game. "First of all, flowers always impress a woman, even if she says they don't." He leaned a little closer. "You've just gotta know which ones she really likes."

Maryann liked flowers well enough, outside of the fact that they were just going to die.

The problem was, bringing her flowers would put him in the same pool as every other man who showed up on her doorstep.

He needed to prove he was different. Better.

And he was coming out of the gate a few steps behind.

"You could call her and officially invite her to Moss Creek." Clint leaned back in his seat. "Tell her you want to see her again and give her a specific date you would like for her to be here."

Telling Maryann when he expected to see her seemed a little—

Bossy. And she'd already had too many men dictate how their relationship was going to go. Just like the one who dragged her to the rodeo because it was what made him happy.

That was part of the reason he hadn't tried to force a trip to Moss Creek on her. He didn't want to pressure her into doing something simply because it was what he wanted.

But maybe he erred too far in the wrong direction. Left her without a clear idea of where he stood.

"You could go back to wherever she's at. Take her out on a few more dates. Make sure she's really what you want, and then lay it all out for her."

That was the best idea Clint had come up with so far, but it still seemed off.

He didn't need any more dates to know where he stood or what he wanted.

A week of being miserable without her made that abundantly clear.

"I think you're right. I think I need to go see her again." He needed to show Maryann how serious he was. Because, even though nothing could be farther from the truth, right now it probably seemed like he walked away without looking back.

And all he'd done was look back, mostly through the bottom of a whiskey glass.

Billy lifted one hand, catching the bartender's attention. "Can I get a cup of coffee?"

For the first time since driving out of California he was ready to look forward. Mostly because there might be something to look forward to.

"You got any plans for the weekend?" Billy grabbed the cup of coffee as soon as it was in front of him and started sucking it down, ignoring the scald as it hit his mouth and throat.

He had plans to make. Ones he needed to be sober for.

Clint shot him a grin. "I always have time for a good road trip."

Billy polished off his coffee before ordering another. "I'm thinking I might want to leave out of here Friday night so we get there first thing Saturday morning."

The more he thought about it, the more he knew it was what he wanted to do. What he had to do.

Even if she turned him around and sent him back on his way, he had to at least try. Show Maryann just how serious he was.

About her.

About them.

About what he knew they could be.

CHAPTER THIRTEEN

MARYANN CREPT OUT of her room, making her way quietly down the hall to the bifold doors of the utility closet that housed the washer and dryer. She eased the shuttered doors apart before crouching down to carefully open the dryer, letting out a little breath when the house remained silent.

She was halfway through dragging the contents out and into her laundry basket when the door to Amanda's room opened and she came face to crotch with Jamie, the guy who kept Amanda up most of the night.

She knew this because he kept her up most of the night too.

"Doing some Saturday morning laundry?" He walked past her on his way to the bathroom, appearing completely unbothered by the fact that he was wearing nothing but his briefs and a smile.

Maryann leaned against the dryer, getting as close as possible without actually crawling inside.

Not that it wasn't an option she was willing to consider if his mostly naked groin breached her personal space.

"Yup." She quickly gathered the rest of her clothes before slamming the dryer closed and hustling back to her room, shutting the door in the hopes that it would block out at least a little of whatever sounds were about to start coming from across the hall.

Based on her experience last night, it wouldn't do much, but something was better than nothing.

She switched on the radio of her alarm clock and turned the volume up, adding another layer of safety she desperately needed.

She was happy for Amanda. Jamie seemed to be the nicest guy her roommate had ever brought home, and he genuinely appeared to be interested in her friend.

But given her own current circumstances, facing down a happy couple that seemed attached right out of the gate wasn't at the top of her list of things she wanted to deal with.

Which is why she was doing laundry.

It was the same reason she'd cleaned her room from top to bottom and scrubbed the kitchen within an inch of its life.

She needed the distraction. And after overhearing a conversation between Jamie and Amanda, it also seemed like she should be prepared to figure out a new living arrangement in the near future. Having her things together and ready to go would make that whole process as easy as it could be.

A week ago she might have pulled her friend aside and tried to convince her things were moving too fast, but that was before she met a man she would have happily floored the gas for.

It was too bad he pumped the brakes.

Maryann dumped out the basket of clothes across her mattress, hitting it against her bed with a little too much force, but it felt good to knock out a little frustration.

Maybe she'd take on the bathroom when she was done here. Have at the grout with a toothbrush until she scrubbed away her disappointment.

But disappointment wasn't all she was struggling to work through.

Normally when a relationship came to an end, she was more than ready to move on. And even through what she had with Billy could scarcely be considered a relationship—hell, it was barely an introduction—she was in more pain after only a couple days with him than she'd been after any other breakup.

Not that Billy even really broke up with her. He just sort of...

Left.

And maybe that's why she was struggling so much. There was no closure. No reason given for why he didn't want to see where they would go.

He just gave her a kiss and walked out of her life.

A steady thumping from the other side of her door sent Maryann to her nightstand to crank up the volume of her clock radio, hoping the tune of "Take on Me" would drown out the noise better than the pile of pillows she used last night.

Maryann grabbed at her laundry, quickly folding the pile of socks and underwear before shoving them into her newly organized drawers. As she closed them in, someone knocked on her door.

She tried to keep the cringe off her face as she opened it up, bracing herself for the outline of Jamie's penis through his tighty whities.

She let out a sigh of relief when he was wrapped in one of Amanda's pale pink bathrobes, managing to replace her anticipatory cringe with a hesitant smile. "That color really brings out your eyes."

Hopefully if she encouraged a little more coverage Jamie would get the hint.

He glanced down at the fluffy fabric before giving her a lopsided grin. "Thanks. I thought so too."

Maryann's smile turned a little more genuine. She really did like Jamie. He was a nice guy with a good job and a great head on his shoulders.

He would be good to Amanda, and that was really all anyone could ask for. Someone who would be good to them instead of only worrying about their own wants and needs.

"Did you need something?"

Jamie bobbed his head in a nod as he thumbed toward the living room. "Yeah. There's some guy here. He says he knows you."

Maryann stifled a groan.

Cliff had been calling her every day, begging for a second chance. Swearing he would be more considerate.

Unfortunately, the man didn't get told no often, so it didn't seem to matter how many times she said it, it wasn't registering.

"I'll take care of it." Maryann edged out the door, being careful not to bump against a still mostly naked Jamie.

She marched down the hall, ready to take Cliff on yet again. "Cliff, I don't know how many times I have to say it, I'm just not in—"

The words died off as she came face-to-face with a man who was definitely not Cliff.

"Billy." His name rushed out along with all the air in her lungs.

She never expected to see him again. And definitely not on a Saturday morning while she was still in her pajamas with unbrushed hair. "What are you doing here?"

Billy's eyes held hers for a second before shifting to look down the hall. "Am I interrupting something?"

It would be so easy to give him the truth immediately.

A little too easy.

Maryann crossed her arms over her chest, lifting her chin a little bit at the man scowling toward where Jamie stood outside her room. "I didn't think I would ever see you again."

Billy's eyes slowly dragged from Jamie to meet hers. "I

can see how you would think that." His jaw clenched tight, the muscle in his cheek twitching as he straightened his shoulders. "I shouldn't have left the way I did last weekend."

Had it only been a week? It felt so much longer. "Is that so?"

Billy tipped his head in a nod. "It is."

Maryann lifted her brows, doing her best to stand her ground in the face of the first man she ever felt really listened to her. Saw her. Considered her. "What should you have done?"

"Taken you with me." The answer was immediate and unhesitating.

Also a little shocking. "Taken me with you?"

Billy nodded again. "That's where I think you belong. With me." The tightness in his jaw eased a little. "Just like I think I belong with you."

She was expecting maybe an apology. Possibly an admission that walking away and not calling for a week was bad.

But not this. Not for him to make such a firm and complete declaration.

"But if that's not what you want then I understand." Billy stepped closer. "I know I didn't handle this just right, but I wasn't sure what I was feeling would make sense to you." His eyes moved over her face. "Because it sure as hell didn't make sense to me."

She was speechless. Partly from the shock of seeing him again and partly because she understood exactly what he was saying.

What she felt for him didn't make sense.

It was too easy.

Too simple.

Too uncomplicated.

Her parents' marriage was a mess, and while she didn't think all relationships were like that, she couldn't imagine they were ever easy or simple or uncomplicated.

"I want you to come to Moss Creek with me." Billy continued talking, each bit of honesty softening the firm stance she was trying to take. "I want you to stay there. I want you to meet my family. I want you to meet my friends. I want you to see my ranch." Billy's hand lifted, like he wanted to reach for her, but then dropped back to his side. "And I want you to stay there. I want us to be together. To start a life."

He said it like it would be simple. Like she could literally just choose to go with him right now. This morning. "It's not that easy."

It couldn't be.

"I'm not saying it is." Billy lifted his hand again, but this time it curved against the side of her face, warm and solid and grounding. "But shouldn't some part of this be hard?"

The fact that choosing to be with him would be a complicated process almost made her feel a little better.

She would have to quit her job. Find a new one. Pack up her apartment. Move everything she owned across states. Figure out how to get her car from California to Montana.

And then there was Montana.

"What if I don't like Moss Creek?" It was her biggest fear—maybe her only fear—but a very real one.

Billy's lips pulled into a slow smile. "Then I'll take you anywhere you want to go."

"What about your family's ranch? You're supposed to take that over."

Billy's whole life was waiting for him in Moss Creek. A house. A business. His family. Everything was there.

"I want you more."

How could such a simple statement make it so hard for her to breathe?

She'd gone out with men who couldn't be bothered to give up a restaurant they liked for her, let alone walk away from everything they knew.

Maryann shook her head. "Montana is where you belong." She didn't know anything about the state, outside of what Billy had told her, but there wasn't much that mattered besides the fact that he was there.

And that might just be enough.

She gave him a little smile. "So maybe that's where I belong too."

Billy scooped her up, pulling her close as he spun in a circle, pressing his lips to hers.

Billy's momentum slowed at the loud sound of applause and whistling. When he eased Maryann back to her feet and slowly pulled his lips from hers, she followed his gaze as his attention fixed on their audience at the end of the hall. Amanda forked her fingers between her lips and let out another whistle while Jamie, still in the pink robe, slow-clapped as he smiled their way.

Jamie wiped at a tear leaking from the corner of one eye. "That was beautiful, man."

Billy looked from Jamie to Amanda before turning back to Maryann and lifting his brows.

She smiled up at him. “If you’re jealous I can get you a pink robe of your own.”

Billy’s head tipped back in a burst of laughter. “I’m more of a peach man.” He scooped her up, lifting her into the air before carrying her out the door and down the steps.

Maryann latched onto his neck, holding tight as he crossed the small patch of grass that served as their front yard. “Where are we going?”

“Wherever you want. I already said that.” Billy dropped her feet to the sidewalk and directed her toward his truck.

And the trailer attached to the back of it.

He snagged her hand, linking his fingers with hers as he led her to the rear of the trailer. “I brought you somethin’.”

She peeked into the cab of his truck as they passed, giving the man waiting inside a little wave.

Billy unlatched the hatch on the drop-down door and lifted it up to reveal several flats of flowers of various colors and types, their bright blooms standing out in the darkened interior. “These won’t just die.”

Maryann leaned forward, reaching out to stroke

along one of the petals. "They're perfect." Her eyes lifted to the empty trailer.

He definitely didn't bring that all the way here because of a few flats of flowers.

"I'm glad you like them." Billy lifted her hand to his lips, brushing a kiss across her knuckles. "Now you just have to decide where you want to plant them."

EPILOGUE

"I THINK HE spit up again." Billy's dad turned, showing him his back. "Did he get any on me?"

A chunky streak of white trailed down the back of his father's bright red Christmas sweater, running from the shoulder he had his grandson propped against, all the way down to the hem.

Billy grabbed one of the many receiving blankets scattered around the farmhouse, shaking it open as he rushed to his dad's rescue. "Let's just say it looks like you won't be wearing that sweater at dinner."

He did his best to clean his dad up before folding the blanket to a fresh spot and wiping across Brody's smiling baby face. "You've got to stop puking on your grandpa, buddy. You're gonna ruin every shirt he has."

Lonnie Pace grinned as he passed Brody off to Bill. "I can always buy more shirts." He reached out to tap Brody on the tip of his little nose. "But my first grandbaby will only be little once." He headed for the stairs, pulling off the ruined sweater as he walked. "Don't shake him up while I'm gone."

Bill grabbed a fresh blanket and slung it over his shoulder, hoping it might catch at least a little bit of whatever Brody had left in his stomach.

The amount of vomit that could come from one small human was something he wasn't quite prepared for. Hell, he was prepared for very little of what came with fatherhood, so most of what he'd figured out was trial by fire.

Or in this case, upchuck.

Bill propped Brody against his covered shoulder, gently patting his son's back as they meandered their way into the kitchen where Maryann was helping his mother prepare Christmas dinner.

She'd taken to ranch life like a fish to water, proving time and time again what they both knew from the get-go.

They were meant to be together. Meant to be here, in Moss Creek, running Red Cedar Ranch together and raising babies.

As a team.

Maryann lifted a spoon from the pot in front of her and held it out. "Taste this."

Bill immediately did as he was told and opened wide. It didn't matter what it was or how hot it might be, if Maryann wanted him to taste it and tell her it was the best thing he'd ever had, that was what he would do.

Luckily, she was one hell of a cook so it was always the truth.

"That's good." It was milky and creamy and sweet. Almost like a pudding, but not quite. "Real good."

"Alberta McBride that lives over on Churchill gave me her recipe for sugar cream pie and I thought it would be a good addition to our dessert spread." Maryann picked up the pot and emptied the contents out into a pie crust, smoothing the top before sprinkling on a dash of cinnamon.

"I certainly won't complain." Bill bounced Brody a little when he started to fuss. "Anything I can do to help you girls?"

Maryann opened the oven and slid the pie onto the middle rack before setting the timer. "Honestly, the best thing you can do for me is to keep captain pukey pants occupied." She paused at his side, reaching out to smooth across the soft strands of Brody's blonde hair. "But I get it if you need a break."

"Pretty sure this parenting gig doesn't involve breaks." Bill wrapped one arm around Maryann and pulled her close. "I think they put that part in the fine print."

Maryann laughed, circling her arms at his waist as she leaned into him. "That's how they get you." She rested her head on his shoulder, coming nose to nose with their little boy. "But I would have done it anyway. He's pretty cute." She pressed a kiss to Brody's forehead. "Even though everything we own smells like curdled milk."

He definitely agreed. He'd do it all over again in a heartbeat.

Hopefully they'd be luckier than his parents were and have the opportunity.

Brody was one hell of a happy baby. A bit of a puker, but the little guy even did that with a smile on his face. So far the worst part about parenthood was all the extra laundry and mopping they had to do because of the constant spit up.

Bill's dad strode into the kitchen, tucking in his fresh shirt as he went to where his mother worked on cutting dumplings. "You're making enough food to feed an army."

Bill's mom smiled softly as her warm gaze turned to Brody. "I figure I need to practice since soon we're going to have a big strapping boy here ready to eat us out of house and home."

“Just one?” Lonnie nudged Bill with an elbow as he passed. “I figure we'll end up with a whole damn football team before it's all said and done.”

Vera Pace shot her husband a glare. “Don't pressure them, Lonnie. Let them get their feet under them with this one.” Her lips lifted at the corners. “Then we can start pressuring them.”

"I think a football team is a little bit of a stretch." Bill gently bounced his baby boy, rocking from side to side as Brody yawned. “Maybe a hockey team.”

Maryann rolled her eyes, giving him a little bump with her hip as she stepped away. “You're delivering half of them then.”

Bill laughed long and loud.

It was something he did a lot of these days.

He had everything he'd ever wanted.

A wife who was the perfect person to stand at his side.

A healthy baby boy who might one day want to take on the ranch as his own.

A home filled with love and joy and more happiness than he could shake ten sticks at.

And a future that was much different from the one he'd tried to run from not so long ago.

All he wanted to do now was think of his future. What it had in store for him.

For them. For the ranch.

It was crazy to think that at one point he'd done everything he could to avoid the very thing that brought him more joy than he ever could have imagined.

On one hand it made him feel like a fool.

But if he hadn't joined the rodeo and ventured out on his own he never would have met Maryann.

And he'd do it all over again if it meant finding her and having the same little boy drooling on the shoulder of his thermal shirt and spitting up all over everything he owned.

The only thing he regretted was not bringing Maryann home with him after that first weekend.

He'd missed out on a whole week with her because of it, and that was time he'd never get back.

Maryann frowned as Brody yawned again, one little

fist coming up to rub at his eye. “He should probably get a nap before dinner.”

“I think I can handle a nap.” He shot her a wink and a grin as he worked his way toward the back stairs. “I might take one myself.”

He’d been up most of the night with Brody, walking the floors while his son worked out a wicked case of gas, kicking his legs and fussing until well after four in the morning.

"You probably need a nap worse than he does." Maryann's smile turned soft. "I'll make sure you're awake before we start to eat."

Bill carried Brody up the back staircase, making his way to the second largest of the six bedrooms on the upper floor.

His parents built the house shortly after they were married, thinking they'd be able to fill it with kids.

It hadn't worked out that way for them, but maybe he'd have better luck.

Maybe one day all those bedrooms would be full of the family he planned to build with Maryann.

Hell, maybe one day he'd get to play with his own grandchildren in these halls.

As he tucked Brody in and stretched out on the bed, it was impossible not to think about what was to come.

It had been that way since Maryann came into his life. It was impossible not to think about the future and, after so many years of living in the moment, he was more than ready to settle down and start making plans.

Plans that would involve any dream Maryann could

come up with. If she wanted it, he would bend over backward to make sure he gave it to her, whether it was babies or vacations or free time and a good night's sleep.

All that mattered was that she would have whatever it took to make her happy.

Because she'd already given him enough to keep him happy for five lifetimes.

Made in the USA
Monee, IL
25 May 2023

34613117R00092